Border Walls
A Musical About Redbeard
of the Rio Grande

Script, lyrics, score, and illustrations by
Milo Kearney

Border Walls
A Musical About Redbeard of the Rio Grande
Second Edition
All Rights Reserved
Copyright © 2003 - 2017, Milo Kearney
Illustrations © 2003 - 2017, Milo Kearney
–All rights reserved, used with permission
Pukiyari Publishers

ISBN-13: 978-1-63065-082-7
ISBN-10: 1-63065-082-X

PRINTED IN THE UNITED STATES OF AMERICA
www.pukiyari.com

Cast of Characters

1. Juan "Cheno" Cortina (heroic, intense, easily-angered)
2. Estefana Goseascochea de Cortina (Juan's mother, charming, self-possessed)
3. Adolphus Glaevecke, Juan's personal enemy (overbearing, determined)
4. Mrs. Concepción Glaevecke, Adolphus' wife & Juan's cousin (excitable, flighty)
5. Charles Stillman (pragmatic, dry, money-obsessed)
6. Dr. John (Rip) Ford, Texas Ranger (dignified, with a strong Texas twang)
7. Rafaela Cortez, Cortina's second wife (determined, prim & proper, shrill)
8. Tomás Cabrera, one of Cortina's cowhands (fat, inebriated, jolly, funny, sloppy)
9. Marshall Bob Shears (serious, pushy)
10. Cortina's girlfriend (brazen, loud, sarcastic)
11. Tomás Cabrera's side-kick (just like him)
12. Street singer
13. Narrator

Cameo Appearances (1 actress and 2 actors can repeat in these parts):

14. La llorona
15. Mexican soldier
16. U.S. soldier
17. Curandera (poorly-dressed old hag with a resonating cackle & grey hair)
18. El Zorro (Salomon Pico)
19. Governor Servando Canales of Tamaulipas
20. Sheriff Brito
21. Cortina's young third wife

Dancers and singers in the "Square Dance of the Civil Wars" and again as anonymous old people in the "Waltz of Old Age" (can use 7 of the cameo appearance roles plus Cortina's second wife Rafaela):

1. U.S. President Abraham Lincoln
2. Mrs. Mary Todd Lincoln
3. Mexican President Benito Juárez (**sings**)
4. Mrs. Margarita Maza de Juárez
5. Confederate President Jefferson Davis (**sings**)
6. Mrs. Jefferson Davis
7. Mexican Emperor Maximiliano (**sings**)
8. Mexican Empress Carlota

Order of Scenes

Act I

1. The Dean Porter Park Resaca, Brownsville (1850s)
[Street singer and Chorus sing the "Corrido of Juan Cortina"]
2. Living room of Estefana Cortina's Rancho del Carmen ranch house west of the site of the future Brownsville (March 1846)
3. The battlefields of Palo Alto & Resaca de la Palma (May 1846)
4. Church of the Immaculate Conception, Brownsville (1850)
5. Brownsville's Washington Park (1852)
6. A Brownsville cantina (1858)
7. Gabriel Catchell's Coffee Shop, Brownsville (July 1859)
[Chorus sings "La Curandera"]
8. A curandera's back yard, Brownsville (August 1859)
 [Chorus sings "Ballad of Cortina the Hero"]
9. Street in front of Adolphus Glaevecke's house, Brownsville (September 1859)
10. Camp of the Brownsville Tigers outside Brownsville (December 1859)
11. Cortina's camp south of the Rio Grande, across from Rio Grande City (March 1860)

Act II

[The Square Dance of the American and the Mexican civil wars (1860s)]

1. The Matamoros headquarters of General Juan Cortina, Governor of Tamaulipas (1863)
2. In front of Estefana Cortina's Rancho del Carmen ranch house west of Brownsville (April 1864)
3. Street singer recites the "Poem of the End of the Civil Wars" (1864-1866)
4. Governor Servando Canales' office in Matamoros (April 1877)
5. Adolphus Glaevecke's house in Brownsville (Monday 18 August 1879)
[Street singer and Chorus sing and couples dance the "Waltz of Old Age"]
6. A restaurant banqueting room in Matamoros (1890)
[Street singer and Chorus sing a reprise of the "Corrido of Juan Cortina"]

ACT ONE

BORDER WALLS
A MUSICAL ABOUT REDBEARD OF THE RIO GRANDE

Script, lyrics, and music by Milo Kearney

(With musical notation help by Kathleen Anzak
and with the tune for the "Waltz of Old Age" written by Vivian Kearney)

OVERTURE

@@@@@@@@@@@@@

Narrator: Welcome to our presentation of *Red Beard of the Rio Grande*. This musical play is a historical account of episodes in the settlement of Brownsville, Texas, back in the early 19th century. Today, we think of Brownsville as a peaceful and uneventful town, but this was not always the case. Life was risky then. There could be a beautiful society wedding on one day, and the next day gun-toting insurgents could shoot up the town. Juan Cortina, "Red Beard," played a pivotal role in the history of the Lower Rio Grande Valley. During the Mexican-American War, he fought the American take-over of the north bank of the Rio Grande, and he spent much of the rest of his life fighting for one cause or another along the border. This is the man and these are the times we now call to our stage. In the opening scene, La Llorona, the weeping spirit of the Mexican people, arises from a resaca, where she has drowned herself in grief.

@@@@@@@@@@@@@@

Act I, Scene I – The Porter Park Resaca, Brownsville. La Llorona of Brownsville's Dean Porter Park Resaca rises out of the water, soaking wet and sobbing.

La Llorona [screaming]: Aieee! [with a Mexican accent] Oh, my children, what have they done to you? My dear Mexican children of the Lower Rio Grande! Oh, my children! When your Anglo father first came to our soil, he took me as his Mexican beauty. He promised to care for me, and for you. But then he turned against our people, our country. He rallied to a new flag, and to a new culture. He left us living in rags, despised and scorned. And so, suffocated by my tears, I drowned in grief. Who will revenge us? Juan Cortina, you are my only hope. Come to the rescue of your people. Help us! Help us! [Curtain]

Song: The Corrido of Juan Cortina

(Sung by the street singer with guitar and Chorus with piano)

Sung by the Street Singer:

All you people, come and rally
to the song of Juan Cortina,
from the Rio Grande Valley,
toast of rancho and cantina.

Sung by the Chorus:

Red his beard, and red his glare,
and red his temper for a fight.
Red the blood when anger flared,
shed defending what seemed right.

When divisions tore the land,
and ground our noses in the dirt,
Juan Cortina led his band
so to defend our homes and worth.

Where does truth lie in this story?
Who is right, and who is wrong?
Will the problem find solution
at the ending of his song?

@@@@@@@@@@@@@@@@@

Narrator: In the next scene, Juan Cortina and his mother are entertaining Charles Stillman and the Glaeveckes at their ranch house near the Rio Grande.

@@@@@@@@@@@@@@@@@

Act I, Scene 2 – At Señora Cortina's Rancho del Carmen living room on the north side of the Rio Grande across from Matamoros (March, 1846). Mrs. Cortina is serving coffee to Charles Stillman, Adolphus Glaevecke, Mrs. Concepción Glaevecke, and Mrs. Cortina's son Juan ("Cheno") Cortina.

Mrs. Glaevecke (with an enthusiastic but refined Mexican accent): You are such a wonderful hostess, prima!

Mrs. Cortina (with a refined Mexican accent, jumping up and grabbing a dish of pastries): Oh! Would anyone like some more coffee and *pan dulce*?

Cortina (with a Mexican accent, pushing her back down in her chair): No! We're all stuffed, Mamá. You should know not to egg her on, Concepción.

Glaevecke (with a strong German accent): Ve weally have had enough, tank you, zough.

Mrs. Cortina: Well, our community has become far more civilized than when I was a girl.

Stillman (with a Connecticut accent): You can bank on that.

Mrs. Glaevecke: Isn't that the tr… [She is drowned out by Glaevecke speaking at the same time]

Glaevecke: Ze vunderful growth is mostly your doink, Charles; your's and your papa's. Your shipping business has been a weal help.

Stillman: Although you, Señora Cortina, were the only one brave enough to stay on your ranch when the Comanches swept over the north bank of the river.

Mrs. Cortina (pointing to her son): Well, Juan's extermination of the Karankawas made the other Indians respect us. When he was little, we couldn't keep him in school, even when his father was alive. He was always running off, or getting expelled for starting fights. And when he was a teenager, he got into constant scrapes with his gang of wild cowboys.

Cortina (with a Mexican accent): Yes, and when I misbehaved, you made me hunt for my own food!

Mrs. Cortina: All the same, your spunk saved us from the Indians.

Mrs. Glaevecke: But now I'm so scared by these rumors of an American invasion. *Ay, ¡me dan tanto miedo!* What do you think is going to happen, Mr. Stillman?

Stillman: War is inevitable, Señora Glaevecke, since the U.S. is claiming the Rio Grande River as the U.S.-Mexican boundary.

Cortina (bursting in before the word "boundary" is out of Stillman's mouth): That's outrageous! The Nueces River has always been the dividing line between Texas and the rest of Mexico.

Stillman: Right on the money! That's why Polk could send an army here, and be sure that the Mexican forces would attack it.

Mrs. Glaevecke: Oh, so that's… [she is overridden by Glaevecke again]

Glaevecke: Zen Polk could claim a Mexican invasion of American soil, and Congress would have to declare war.

Cortina: Such a development would test the loyalty to Mexico of you two men, wouldn't it? You both came here from the United States, although you, Adolphus, were originally from Germany.

Glaevecke [speaking in German]: *So was*! *(pronounced Zo vass!)*

Mrs. Cortina: Where are your manners, Juan? Remember that these gentlemen have long been an important part of our town. Please show respect.

Mrs. Glaevecke: And remember, *primo*, that my dear Adolphus is now part of our family. Shame on you for questioning his loyalty!

[A Mexican soldier enters left.]

Mexican soldier (with a Mexican accent): Señora, word has just arrived that an American army under General Zachary Taylor is moving into Point Isabel. We have been invaded.

Mrs. Glaevecke: *O, Diosito, ¡no!*

Mexican soldier: Mr. Stillman, I have orders to escort you to board a ship bound for the United States. You must come with me at once. [They exit.]

Cortina: Mother, I am going to join General Arista's troops. And you, Adolphus?

Glaevecke: My first duty is to home and family. Come, Concepción, we must get back to ze wanch.

Cortina: And then what? You're not going to help the Americans, are you?

Glaevecke: *Donnerwetter*! [pronounced Donervetter]

Mrs. Cortina: Juan, I didn't bring you up this way! Yes, fight to protect our land, but don't insult our guest.

Cortina: All right. Good-by, mother. [All exit except for Mrs. Cortina, who sinks into a chair.]

Mrs. Cortina: God protect us! [She crosses herself.]

@@@@@@@@@@@@

Narrator: The first two battles of the Mexican-American War took place in May of 1846. In this scene, the Mexicans, including Juan Cortina, try to hold the line at Palo Alto. Cortina's anger flares toward the gringos, and especially towards Adolphus Glaevecke, whom he feels is a traitor. Glaevecke is selling beef to the U.S. troops and is acting as a scout and a secret courier. During the battle of Palo Alto, the U.S. troops use a smoke screen to encircle the Mexican troops, who retreat to the Resaca de la Palma.

@@@@@@@@@@@@

Act I, Scene 3 [Optional] – On the battlefields, first of Palo Alto and then of the Resaca de la Palma (May 1846). [Cortina and a Mexican soldier are shooting off and on. **Music of "Cortina Snippet # 1** plays first]

Mexican soldier: We need to stop the gringos here at Palo Alto.

Cortina: I'll die in the effort if I have to, but I hope I can live long enough to get even with that traitor Adolphus Glaevecke. As soon as he got back to his ranch, the bastard offered his services to the invaders. He's not only selling beef to the U.S. troops. He's also acting as their scout and secret courier. He's been a busy little beaver, but he'll pay.

Mexican soldier: Look! That grass fire started by the cannons is really getting out of control.

Cortina: I can't see the Americans with all that smoke.

Mexican soldier: Do you think they're using the smokescreen to circle behind us?

Cortina: I bet they are. And look, General Arista is calling us to retreat. ¡Vámonos! [They exit right. Then Glaevecke and an American soldier cross the stage from left to right, talking as they go.]

Glaevecke: Sch n! Zat smoke vas just vat ve needed. Let me show you a good woute around the fire back to ze main woad south.

[They exit right. Cortina and a Mexican soldier enter left, walking backwards.]

Mexican soldier: Now we're getting signals to stop here.

Cortina: Good choice! The Resaca de la Palma is a natural spot to hold the line.

Mexican soldier: But here they come again, right behind us. And wouldn't you know it, there's Adolphus Glaevecke with them.

Cortina: ¡Maldito sea! He led them right to where we were going.

Mexican soldier: And they're getting ready to charge. Watch out! Here they come! [he turns suddenly toward the audience and fires his gun fiercely]

[Curtain]

@@@@@@@@@@@@

Narrator: It is now 1850, two years after the U.S. defeat of Mexico, and Juan Cortina is marrying Rafaela, his second wife.

@@@@@@@@@@@@

Act I, Scene 4 – In Brownsville's Cathedral of the Immaculate Conception (1850) [First Cortina and Rafaela, standing in the center of their guests, holding hands, she in a wedding dress, sing, and then all the watching guests sing…]

Song: Wedding Processional

(Sung by Rafaela, Cortina, and Guests)

Rafaela: When two people get married,
they both have the perfect mate,
and, since they are so flawless,
they find that things turn out just

Cortina: so hard to readjust to
When they do everything wrong.
At least, they have each other,
And their time together is

Rafaela: short, as everything's too rushed.
There's too few hours in the day,
but, with family input, then
everything's going their

Cortina: nerves to quickly unravel,
They find they're losing their rest.
Still, they're young and they're healthy,
So everything works for the

[then Cortina and Rafaela dance while the guests take over the singing.]

Women guests: worst, when sickness attacks them,
and they can't sleep through the night.
It's good they've no disagreements,
So everything turns out just

Men guests: wrong, when they blame each other,
and snap and bicker and shove,
but they'll solve all their problems,
if they're really and truly in love.

Everybody: If they're really and truly in love.

[During this line, Cortina and Rafaela stop dancing and hug and kiss. The guests then congratulate the couple and begin to exit, including an obvious flirt--the later mistress of Cortina—who looks back seductively as she leaves. Cortina takes note of her.]

Mrs. Cortina: You've been through some rough times, Cheno, with your first wife's death, and our losing the war of the American Intervention. But this is a new start for you, with your new bride in your new country, as an American.

Cortina: Excuse me one minute. [He exits, talking to the guests.]

Mrs. Cortina (to Rafaela): Well, my dear, you have grabbed the bull by the horns. So hold on tight.

Rafaela (with a Mexican accent): I know what people are saying. They say that Juan is too wild to be tamed. But don't worry. I know how to handle Cheno. [Rafaela sings this song…]

Song: He'll Always be Mine (waltz)
(Sung by Rafaela Cortez)

He's had other women. I know what they say.
They all think I'm only his choice for today.
But I've got my eye on him. He won't get away.
He'll always be, always be, always be, always be,
always be, always be mine.

His previous women were slow on their feet.
To hold such a man you don't dare miss a beat.
But he's now met his match, and so need I repeat?
He'll always be, always be, always be, always be,
always be, always be mine.

In musical chairs, players come to a stop.
A ball's bouncing comes to an end.
The spinning can last just so long with a top,
Then comes to a halt once again.

The life of a hero must never be dull.
His partner must be someone special as well.
For the rest of his life he'll be under my spell.
He'll always be, always be, always be, always be,
always be, always be mine.

Mrs. Cortina: That's the spirit, my dear. Now you stick to it.

[Curtain]

@@@@@@@@@@@@

Narrator: The next scene takes place in 1852 in Washington Park in the new town of Brownsville, which has been founded by Charles Stillman.

@@@@@@@@@@@@

Act I, Scene 5 – In Brownsville's Washington Park in 1852. [Couples and families stroll or sit on benches. Glaevecke is reading a newspaper on one bench, when Stillman enters and greets him, and sits down beside him].

Stillman: Well, Glaevecke, we've seen quite a few changes since we had coffee at Mrs. Cortina's house right before the war, haven't we?

Glaevecke: Zat cwazy war weally had us sveating until ze Americans von.

Stillman: I sure was. I would have been sent into exile, if I hadn't managed to escape. It cost me five weeks hiding out with friends until it was safe to show my face again.

Glaevecke: And when zat *verdammte* Mexican patrol caught me dwiving some of my cattle to ze American camp, zey condemned me to be shot, and I tought I vas a goner.

Stillman: I knew that Mrs. Cortina would stand up for you as her cousin's husband. And she'd nursed so many Mexican soldiers back to health that it's no wonder that the Mexican authorities let you go.

Glaevecke: *Ja*, but Juan was so mad, I thought he vas going to shoot me himself.

Stillman: Well, that's old business. Now if we can just get people to invest in my new town of Brownsville, we'll all be the better for it.

Glaevecke: It <u>is</u> a vunderful town you've started. And it vas womantic to name ze main stweet for your vife, Elizabeth.

Stillman: She <u>was</u> happy about that.

Glaevecke: And it vas also vewy nice to name another stweet St. Francis to honor your Papa.

Stillman: Well, I owe him quite a bit.

Glaevecke: And it's vewy fitting that one of ze main stweets should be named St. Charles after yourself.

Stillman: It <u>is</u> a dandy town, isn't it?

[They sing…]

Song: The Corrido of Brownsville
(Sung by Stillman and Glaevecke)

My dear Rio town of Brownsville,
with resacas twisting, turning,
and your home fires brightly burning.
You're just where I want to be.
On the Border, by the sea,
You really do look good to me.
Palm trees stand beside your roads,
where flocks of birds have their abodes.

My dear Rio town of Brownsville,
with warm breezes softly blowing,
and your bright strong sun aglowing
over where I want to be.
No more snow, and no more ice,
I'd choose you without thinking twice.

No more walking in the cold.
Winter's no wonderland when you are old.

My dear Rio town of Brownsville,
with your sage and cactus blooming,
and your chacalacas pluming,
I am where I want to be.

[Cortina and his mother enter, strolling.]

Glaevecke: Ze only dark cloud is zat pest Cortina. Ze town needs law and order, and protection from trouble-makers like him. [He exchanges angry looks with Cortina.]

[Stillman and Glaevecke stand up and walk off, nodding to the Cortinas as they pass them.]

Cortina: They're triumphant now, but I swear they'll pay.

Mrs. Cortina: Now calm down, Cheno. Things are bad, but we have to change with the times, and adapt to American citizenship. We remain leading ranchers. And I'm still needed in the local society.

[She sings…]

Song: Society Queen of Brownsville
(Sung by Cortina's Mother and Cortina)

Mrs. Cortina:

I've been society queen for years now.
I set the tone, as you will allow.
I've held on to my position somehow.
I'm still the lady who shows them how.

[Cortina's mother persuades a reluctant Cortina to dance a type of flamenco with her during the chorus.]

Mrs. Cortina (dancing around Cortina): I'm still society Queen of Brownsville.

Cortina (clapping in time): Todavía eres la reina.

Mrs. Cortina: I'm still society Queen of Brownsville.

Cortina: Eres la reina de la sociedad.

Mrs. Cortina:

Envious people are left to stew,
one step behind me, or even two.
They would replace me, that much is true,
but they just don't know what they should do.

[Chorus repeats with flamenco dance]

Mrs. Cortina (dancing around Cortina): I'm still society Queen of Brownsville.

Cortina (clapping in time): Todavía eres la reina.

Mrs. Cortina: I'm still society Queen of Brownsville.

Cortina: Eres la reina de la sociedad.

Mrs. Cortina:

So don't you fret about nasty schemes.
Such people often go to extremes,
but they will never upset all our dreams.
We've remained much stronger than it seems.

[While the Cortinas dance, the people in the park sing the chorus]:

Women: You're still society Queen of Brownsville.

Men (clapping in time): Todavía eres la reina.

Women: You're still society Queen of Brownsville.

Men: Eres la reina de la sociedad.

[Mrs. Cortina ends her dance with a flourish, one hand in the air, on the last note, while Cortina gestures toward her.]

@@@@@@@@@@@

Narrator: At a Brownsville cantina, in 1858, Cortina and his ranch hand Tomás Cabrera discuss the victory of Cortina's choice for sheriff in a recent election.

@@@@@@@@@@@

Act I, Scene 6 – A Brownsville cantina (1858). [Cortina enters right and is greeted by a drunken, slurred-speeched, and hiccupping, but smiling, corpulent, sloppily-dressed, and merry Tomás Cabrera, who speaks with a sing-songy *chilango* accent, one of his cowhands, and Cabrera's similar & equally drunk and happy cowhand side-kick at the bar. Cabrera and his side-kick sport big moustaches and are wearing huge sombreros and ponchos. The two cowhands look at each other and laugh a lot as they mumble together and drink. Cabrera waves his beer bottle as he talks.]

Cabrera: *Hola, Jefe. ¿Qué tal*? Here's a cerveza for you. [Cortina joins them at their table.] How did the election go?

Cortina: Our man won. James Brown is the new sheriff.

Cabrera: *¡Que bueno*! With that and with your brother José MarPa still tax collector, we're doing pretty well.

[Glaevecke enters.]

Cortina: I'm a North American now, and I'm going to win by their rules.

Glaevecke: You von because you packed ze election, Cortina. Don't spwain your arm patting yourself on ze back.

Cortina: You're mad because I'm doing so much better at ranching.

Glaevecke: It is weally funny, isn't it, zat my herds are dvindling at exactly ze same rate as your herds are growing? You're not a successful businessman, you're a cattle wustler!

Cabrera: [calming down Cortina, who'd grabbed his gun] As if there's any difference between a businessman and a crook here on the Rio Grande! Come on!

Cabrera's side-kick (laughing): Yeah!

Glaevecke: You and your Mexican patwiot buddies had betta not push your luck too far. You might find you are standing on a slippewy slope.

Cortina: Slippery slope, is it? [He sings...}

Song: Slippery Slope
(Sung by Cortina)

This scoffer tells me, "If you dare,
admit your errors fair and square.
I'll prove that you have been a dope
to be standing on a slippery slope."

Slippery slope, slippery slope.
I'm not standing on any slippery slope.
My feet are firm any way I turn,
because I'm standing on the rock of fairness.

We Mexicans are told to be
polite and humble constantly,
but we'll speak up, as you will note,
without falling down a slippery slope.

Slippery slope, slippery slope.
I'm not standing on any slippery slope.
My feet are firm any way I turn,
because I'm standing on the rock of fairness.

You see, our cause is not built on sand.
Its prospects stand on solid land.
Our trust's not blind, and so our hope
is not slippery or built on a slope.

Slippery slope, slippery slope.
I'm not standing on any slippery slope.
My feet are firm any way I turn,
because I'm standing on the rock of fairness.

Slippery slope, slippery slope.
I'm not standing on any slippery slope.
Just think it through, the light will come to you.
You'll see I'm standing on the rock of fairness. [end of song]

Cortina: Ironic, isn't it, that you were doing better when we were under Mexico? Do you think you backed the wrong side in the war?

Glaevecke: Zat's it, isn't it? You hate being Amewican. Vy don't you just woll up your sleeves and help to make zis a good countwy?

[Cortina and Glaevecke both sit down to drink at tables on the two sides of the stage, with Cabrera sitting beside Cortina, and shout insults back and forth, as follow…]

Cortina: The Anglo only lives to work.
Glaevecke: Ze Mexican is lazy.
Cortina: No time for fun, he is a jerk.
Glaevecke: No time for work, he's cwazy.

Cortina: The Anglo's always on the run,
Glaevecke: Ze Mexican's all tradition.
Cortina: He only thinks of what's to come.
Glaevecke: He's lacking in ambition.

Glaevecke: Ze Mexican has no initiative.
Cortina: The Anglo chases wealth.
Glaevecke: He only tinks of family.
Cortina: He only thinks of self.

Glaevecke: Mexicans are sunk in superstition.
Cortina: Anglos are all the same.
Glaevecke: Zey can't progress; zey can't transition.
Cortina: They'll sell their souls for gain.

Glaevecke (jumping up): You just can't accept zat you live in the good old United States now. Vel, you had better love it or leave it. [yelling] If you cannot be a loyal American, why don't you get the hell out and go live in Mexico? [Glaevecke exits right.]

Cabrera: Lousy gringo! Let <u>him</u> be the one to get out, back to Yankeeland, or better yet all the way back to Germany, and leave us Mexicans with our home again. Right, boss?

Cortina: Yeah. [pause] I <u>think</u> so. But since the war, sometimes I'm confused about it. What am I really, Mexican or American?

Song <u>OR</u> Monologue: Am I A Mexican or an American

(Sung by Cortina <u>OR</u> spoken by Cortina with the music behind him)

Cortina (continuing): Am I a Mexican or an American
when all is said and done?
Am I a Mexican or an American?
I would like to know which one.
For breakfast I eat my eggs with tortilla,
while reading the paper *en la lengua española*
and humming a song *en la moda ranchera*.

So, if I walk like a Mexican,
and I talk like a Mexican,
then I must be a Mexican. Right?

Cabrera: (shrugging) "¡Sí!"

Cabrera's Side-kick (echoing Cabrera): "¡Sí!"

Cortina:
Then I must be a Mexican.
On the other hand…
Am I a Mexican or an American,
when all is said and done?
Am I a Mexican or an American?
I'd like to know which one.

I buy U.S. goods as a general rule.
My daughter attends an American school.
I have freedoms from punishments
unusual or cruel.
So, if I walk like an American,
and I talk like an American,
then I must be American. Right?

Cabrera (shrugging, weakly asks) "Yes?"

Cabrera's Side-kick (looking at Cabrera & shrugging): "Yes?"

Cabrera:
Then I must be American.

I'm frijoles and hamburger,
sombrero and jeans,
norteño and Southerner,
such a mixture of things!

So, if I walk like a Mexican,
and talk like an American,
and walk like an American,
and talk like a Mexican,
am I a Mexican?

Or am I American?

Cabrera (confused): I guess you're both, Jefe.

[Cabrera's Side-kick nods encouragingly.]

Cortina: (shouts and slams his fist down in the air) No! I'm still a Mexican!

Cabrera (shouting back, fully exasperated): ¡Caramba!

@@@@@@@@@@@

Narrator: The next scene takes place in Gabriel Catchell's coffee shop in Brownsville in July of 1859. Adolphus Glaevecke and his wife are talking about the feud between Glaevecke and Cortina.

@@@@@@@@@@@

Act I, Scene 7 – Gabriel Catchell's Coffee Shop, Brownsville (July 1859). [Tomás Cabrera is drunk and hiccupping while drinking coffee at one table with his equally drunk side-kick from the previous scene. They laugh and pat each other on the back as they shakily drink their coffee. Glaevecke and his wife are sitting at another table drinking coffee.]

Mrs. Glaevecke: Mi corazón, I wish that this feud between you and Cortina would stop.

Glaevecke: It's not my fault. [Rip Ford and Marshall Bob Shears enter right.] But here are two lawmen who vil help to get Cortina under control. [Glaevecke stands up.] Ford! Shears! Come join us.

Ford and Shears: Good-day, Glaevecke. Good-day, Mrs. Glaevecke. [The men shake hands and sit down.]

Glaevecke: I vas just commenting how lucky ve are to haf such men as you in Bwonsfil. Ve especially owe a lot to you, Dr. Ford. A medical doctor, a politician, and leader of the Texas Wangers. Vat can you not do?

Mrs. Glaevecke: And you have set such a lovely example as vestryman at our Church of the Advent.

Glaevecke: And, by golly, you haf taught ze Mexicans vat-for. Ve ver all amazed ven you led your boys across the wiver and made Matamowos bwing ze tariffs back down.

Shears: That put the fear of the Texas Rangers into them, didn't it? I hear tell that Mexican mothers warn their children to behave or the "rinches" will get them. You've really earned your nickname of Rip for "Rest in Peace" for all the bad guys you've sent to an early grave. Well done!

Cabrera (in a mocking tone, but with slurred speech punctuated by hiccups, walking over to their table with his coffee cup in his hand): Well done! Well done! [Cabrera's side-kick laughs approvingly from his table, nodding on Cabrera's assertions.]

Ford (in a strong West Texas accent): Our conversation is none of your business.

Cabrera: While you're bragging, Ford, why don't you mention how Richard King formed his King Ranch by paying you and your "rinches" bonuses to murder ranchers and then intimidate their widows into selling cheap.

Shears: That's enough from you. Shut up and sit down!

Cabrera: And you call us Mexicans liars and thieves! *¡Pinche Malinche*! [Cabrera gestures with his coffee cup in his hand, and spills his coffee on Mrs. Glaevecke, who screams and jumps up.]

Mrs. Glaevecke: You've spilled coffee all over me! You've ruined my beautiful new dress! [She runs to the side of the stage trying to clean her dress.]

Glaevecke: *Dummkopf! Drecksache!*

Shears: O.K., buster. That's it! You're under arrest. [Shears tries to handcuff Cabrera, who vigorously resists, with Cabrera's side-kick getting drunkenly in the way as well. A scuffle ensues in which Shears hits Cabrera several times on the head with his pistol butt. At that point, Cortina enters, and witnesses Shear's actions.]

Cortina: What's going on in here?

Ford: A drunk has made a scene. The Marshall is arresting him.

Cortina: This man works for me. I'll take him back to my ranch. [Cortina pulls a nodding Cabrera behind him, & Cabrera's side-kick takes refuge there as well.]

Shears: You stay out of this, Cortina. This is a matter for the law.

Cortina: Look here, squint eyes, don't you get high and mighty with me. This is just a poor vaquero who's had too much to drink. [Cabrera nods and drunkenly shakes his finger at Shears.]

Shears: What is it to you, you damned Mexican?

[Cortina pushes Cabrera out the door, whips out his pistol, and shoots Shears in the shoulder, while Mrs. Glaevecke screams. Ford rushes to help the fallen and bleeding Shears, while Cortina holds his pistol on Ford and Glaevecke and backs out fast with Cabrera.]

Glaevecke (shouting): Cortina, you just ended your life here in Bwonsfil. You are finished! [Curtain.]

@@@@@@@@@@@@

Narrator: The next scene involves a curandera. Theoretically, a curandera is a healer using herbs and magic, while a bruja is a witch, using supernatural powers for selfish and often nefarious ends. However, in actuality, the line between the two types of figures is often blurred. Juan Cortina has hired a curandera to help him learn what the future holds. To give Cortina advice, she has decided to conjure up the spirit of the still-living El Zorro from California through the process of bilocation. In bilocation, the spirit is said to move to a different location, while the body sleeps at home.

@@@@@@@@@@@@

Act I; Scene 8 – A curandera's jacal. [The curandera is bending in the dark over a cauldron boiling on a fire, and throws objects into it.]

Men's Chorus (sitting hunched over around the stage, in the dark, covered in black robes, and writhing around) sings…

Song: "La Curandera"
(Male Chorus, with piano and flute accompaniment)

Ooo-ooo-ooo-ooo-ooo.
Curandera, come and cast your spell.
You've found your niche in Brownsville very well.
Place bound chickens on your altar,
light glass candles, do not falter.
We'll listen to the fates you tell.
Ooo-ooo-ooo-ooo-ooo-ooo-ooo-ooo-ooo.

Ooo-ooo-ooo-ooo-ooo.

You draw out fever using just an egg.
You can affect an eye, an arm, a leg.
Not a bad witch, you're a good one,
or is this an oxymoron?
Are you the healer or the plague?
Ooo-ooo-ooo-ooo-ooo-ooo-ooo-ooo-ooo.

Ooo-ooo-ooo-ooo-ooo.
Tell us, mirror, what the future holds.
Now show Cortina as the years unfold.
Will his fight for right advance?
Tell us what should be his stance,
For he is waiting to be told.
Ooo-ooo-ooo-ooo-ooo-ooo-ooo-ooo-ooo.   [End of song]

[Cortina enters left.]

Curandera (in a cracked old cackling voice): Hola, Juan! Everything's ready.

Cortina: I want advice. Should I submit myself to arrest and a trial for shooting the Marshall? Or should I fight back?

Curandera: My voices are telling me that you need to talk to a Californio who has already stood at the same crossroad and made his choice. I'm calling up his spirit so he can speak to you.

Cortina: You're calling him from the dead?

Curandera: No, he is very much alive.

Cortina: Then how can you bring him over here?

Curandera: With my powers of bi-location. The man is asleep in his bed in California, but his spirit is flying here. There's just one final ingredient needed to carry this off, which you promised to bring. Remember?

Cortina: Here's your money. [Cortina takes out his wallet, and hands over some bills. Then he sits on the ground.]

Curandera (waving her hand over the cauldron):

El Zorro, come and tell your story.
Was your effort worth the worry?
Tell us how you formed your band.
Would you do it all again?

[A ghostly El Zorro partly emerges from the darkness..]

Curandera: Spirit, identify yourself.

El Zorro:

Hola! hail! Juan Cortina, amigo!
I'm Salomón Pico, called El Zorro.
My family, too, were great rancheros,
until land grabbers turned our joy to sorrow.
Deprived of land and dignity,
I was treated with inhumanity.
They raped and murdered my sweet wife,
taking all I had in life.
So I formed an insurgent band,
and robbed and killed across the land.
I taught my enemies new fears,
and strung my saddle horn with ears.
So your courage, compadre, I invoke.
Help me champion our conquered folk.

[His spirit departs.]

Cortina: What the Californios have done, we Tejanos can do as well. Adios!

[Cortina rushes out left.]

Curandera: Wait! Wait! [pause] You left too fast, you red-bearded hothead. I was going to warn you that El Zorro will be hanged by the Mexican authorities in a few months. If you had only had the patience to hear me out! Well, [she cackles loudly] so much the worse for you! [She cackles again, uproariously.]

[Curtain.]

@@@@@@@@@@@@

Between scenes – The Chorus of Mexican-American admirers sings the "Ballad of Cortina the Hero," while Cortina walks among the singers, shaking their hands. They pat him on the back and smile at him. However, Glaevecke and Stillman frown and turn their backs on him.

Song: The Ballad of Cortina the Hero
(Sung by the whole chorus)

What would we do without a hero?
What would our poor world be?
Would we have a life worth living?
Would we still have liberty?

O Juan Cortina! O Juan Cortina!
You will dare to fight.
O Juan Cortina! O Juan Cortina!
Struggle for the right.

It's heroes' blood that gives us new life,
for life comes from the blood.
So the blood that spills from heroes
is not just wasted in the mud.

O Juan Cortina! O Juan Cortina!
You will dare to fight.
O Juan Cortina! O Juan Cortina!
Struggle for the right.

We safely sit, thanks to them, at dinner
with all our family.
So when we drink our wine or grape juice,
we drink their blood that made us free.

O Juan Cortina! O Juan Cortina!
You will dare to fight.
O Juan Cortina! O Juan Cortina!

Struggle for the right.

@@@@@@@@@@@@

Narrator: As the sun rises on September 28th of 1859, the streets of Brownsville are filled with danger. A riot breaks out as Cortina and his men raid the town. Shots are fired, citizens run for cover, and shouts of "Viva Cortina!" can be heard. With bullets flying, a house door opens, and Adolphus Glaevecke runs out. He and Marshall Bob Shears begin to shoot back.

@@@@@@@@@@@@

Act I, Scene 9 – (At dawn, 28 September 1859) [A street in front of Glaevecke's house in Brownsville. Shots are fired offstage, and shouts of "Viva Cortina" are heard. A house door opens, and Glaevecke runs out, pulling on his pants, with a double-barrelled shotgun in his hands. Rip Ford runs on stage right, hastily dressed and buttoning his shirt, while holding his pistol.]

Glaevecke: Vat ze hell's going on?

Rip Ford: Cortina and his men are trying to take over the town.

Glaevecke: Verdammte!

[Cortina and Tomás Cabrera run on stage. Glaevecke and Rip Ford take cover behind some bales of hay, shooting at Cortina and his men, who have taken cover on the opposite side of the stage. Shots fire back and forth. Rafaela Cortina enters left and crouches beside Cortina.]

Rafaela: Hold your fire! Stop this shooting at once! Your mother is beside herself with fury, Juan.

Cortina: You've got some nerve, meddling in my affairs. Just because you are my wife doesn't give you the right. Or my mother either.

Rafaela: You've gone too far this time, Juan! Several men have been killed.

Cortina: You're wasting tears for Morris and Neale? They'd both killed Mexicans. It's high time a little justice came to Brownsville. We're giving these bullies a taste of their own medicine.

Rafaela: Bullies? So why was Clemente Reyes killed?

Cortina: He was fighting on the wrong side.

Rafaela: And Viviano García?

Cortina: He was trying to protect the guilty. I really feel bad that he got in the way.

Rafaela: Is this the explanation you're going to give to God?

Cortina: With you and my mother, its always religion.

Rafaela: Just remember that your mother would have been killed by a bullet in the war if it hadn't hit that prayer book she was carrying. Anyways, it might interest you to know that your cousin Miguel Tijerina has gone across the river to ask for Mexican help to stop you. You'd better get out of here fast.

Cortina: I guess you're right. I didn't mean this to be a morning for Mexican tears. [Cortina turns to his men.] O.K., men. Head back to the ranch.

[Cortina, Cabrera, and Rafaela exit shooting to the left.]

Rip Ford: I'm going to round up my Texas Rangers to chase them upriver.

Glaevecke: And I'll get up a posse to help.

[Rip Ford and Glaevecke run off stage.]

[Curtain.]

@@@@@@@@@@@@

Narrator: It is December of 1859. A posse known as the Brownsville Tigers has been formed to chase down Cortina. Rip Ford and Adolphus Glaevecke have captured Tomás Cabrera, Cortina's ranch hand who had created the uproar earlier that year in Catchell's coffee shop.

@@@@@@@@@@@@

Act I, Scene 10 – (December 1859) [Music of Cortina Snippet # 2. Rip Ford enters and meets Glaevecke, who has Tomás Cabrera as a prisoner with his hands tied]

Glaevecke: Rip, I am glad you haf come.

Ford: How did it go for your Brownsville Tigers posse?

Glaevecke: Cortina forced us to go back. But at least ve managed to gwab this troublemaker Tomás Cabrera.

Ford: Cabrera! What do you have to say for yourself?

Cabrera: ¡Viva Cortina! ¡Muerte a los gringos!

Ford: String him up! [Glaevecke takes Cabrera offstage.]

[Curtain.]

@@@@@@@@@@@@

Narrator: Juan Cortina, now based in Mexico, has endangered the steamboat traffic on the Rio Grande. Cortina's mother comes to Cortina's camp to alert him that Rip Ford is planning to cross the river to attack him.

@@@@@@@@@@@@

Act I, Scene 11 – (March 1860) [Cortina's camp south of the Rio Grande, across from Rio Grande City, Texas. Cortina is at his desk, reading papers. His mother enters left.]

Cortina: Mother! What are <u>you</u> doing here?

Mrs. Cortina: I came to warn you. Rip Ford's troops have crossed the river, and are closing in on you. You need to get out of here fast.

Cortina: Don't worry. I've put the fear of Cortina into all the troops that have attacked me so far.

Mrs. Cortina: The truth is, you're lucky to be alive. I heard how Ford attacked you outside of Rio Grande City. You escaped only by swimming your horse across the river, didn't you?

Cortina: But I escaped, and got my forces together again, didn't I? And besides, now I'm on Mexican soil.

Mrs. Cortina: Ford doesn't care where you are. He's already crossed the river after you once, at la Bolsa Bend, and came very close to killing you. I heard that bullets hit your saddle, your reins, your horse's ear, and your belt, and even cut off some of your hair. And now Ford has even more men. If you're smart, you'll get out of here fast.

Cortina [after a pause]: O.K., I'll head south. But don't think that Brownsville has heard the last of me. We'll raid across the river, and rustle their cattle into Mexico until they will wish they had never heard the name of Juan Cortina.

Mrs. Cortina: And what about your mother, who has done so much for you, and loved you so much all of these years? Your actions have separated us.

Cortina: I just can't sit back and watch so much injustice to our people.

Mrs. Cortina: Well, if you're so tenderhearted, what are going to do about your wife and daughter back in Brownsville? Your little girl cries for you all the time. You haven't even sent them a letter.

Cortina: I don't get anything but nagging from Rafaela. And anyway, an outlaw's camp is no place for a wife and daughter.

Mrs. Cortina: When will I ever see you again, my son? [She cries and sings:]

Song: Did It Have To End Like This?

(Sung by Mrs. Cortina)

I loved your happy little face, as you proudly won a race.
When you kids would run and play, you made me laugh my cares away.
Did it have to end like this?

Cowboy leader in your teens. The bravest boy I've ever seen.
Whenever we were in a stew, you would know just what to do.
Did it have to end like this?

I didn't fear as time went by, and I watched you growing tall.
I thought you'de always be close by, and I didn't mind at all.

But now my heart is feeling sore. You won't be with me anymore.
You have cut me off from you. Was it my fault, what did I do?
Did it have to end like this?

Cortina (interrupting her): Stop! That's not a good note for us to part on. Don't worry, Mamá. Everything's going to be all right. [He sings.]

Song: We'll Be Back

(Sung by Juan Cortina)

Do not be sad that I have gone.
Just wait awhile; it won't be long,
And we'll be back, the two of us again.

I had to cut some bad guys down.
They got too pushy in our town,
But we'll be back, the two of us again.

The whole wide world should know we belong to Mexico.
But we'll be back in the spring. We'll do everything.
We'll go out on the town, up one side and down.

So count the hours one by one.
They'll hurry by, so watch them run,

Then we'll be back, the two of us.
They haven't seen the last of us.
No, we'll be back, the two of us again.
We'll be back again. [spoken]: Yeah! [Cortina simultaneously hugs his unhappy mother.]

[Curtain. End of Act I]

ACT TWO

Act II

[A fiddler comes out and plays a few bars of "The Square Dance of the Civil Wars," warming up his fiddle, while dancers prepare for a square dance. While he softly warms up in the background, the Narrator speaks]

@@@@@@@@@@@@@

Narrator: The year is 1863, and a new conflict, the American Civil War, is well underway. The first battle of the war has been fought outside of Rio Grande City, where Confederate supporter Rip Ford won against the pro-Unionist forces, backed by Cortina. By now, a great deal of cotton is being diverted through Brownsville to circumvent the U.S. naval blockade of Confederate ports. The continued flow of cotton hinges on who will be victorious in the simultaneous civil war in Mexico between the Liberal leader Benito Juárez and the Conservative Emperor Maximiliano, with his French army support. The complex interplay between the American and Mexican civil wars might be thought of as a violent square dance between four sets of couples: the Abraham Lincolns [Lincoln bows to the audience and his wife curtseys], the Jefferson Davises [He bows and she curtseys], the Benito Juarezes [He bows and she curtseys], and Emperor Maximiliano and his Empress Carlota [He bows and she curtseys].

@@@@@@@@@@@@@

Song: The Square Dance of the Civil Wars

(Sung by the four Presidents, dancing with their wives. The four presidents' hats identify them by name. Fiddle music with piano.)

Verse 1:

Lincoln: I am President of the United States. [He waves to the audience.]
Benito Juarez: As for me, I'm President of Mexico. [He waves.]
Jefferson Davis: I am President of the Confederacy. [He waves.]
Maximiliano: And I am Emperor of Mexico. [He bows slightly.]

Chorus (sung by the spectators):

So take your partner by the hand, [They take their partners by the hand.]

and do the dosey-doe. [They dosey-doe around their partners.]
Sell cotton while you promenade,
make money as you go. [They promenade.]
Then swing your partner round and round,
prepare your guns to roar, [They swing around their partners.]
and slam into the other sets,
and knock them to the floor. [They slam hard into the opposing set.]

Verse 2:

Maximiliano: I believe you have a right to own your slaves.
Davis: You will understand, we need them to advance.
Juarez: We demand freedom for each one of our folk.
Lincoln: We will not leave this matter just to chance.

Chorus (sung by the spectators):

So take your partner by the hand, [They take their partners by the hand.]
and do the dosey-doe. [They dosey-doe around their partners.]
Sell cotton while you promenade,
make money as you go. [They promenade.]

Then swing your partner round and round,
prepare your guns to roar, [They swing around their partners.]
and slam into the other sets,
and knock them to the floor. [They slam hard into the opposing set.]

Verse 3:

Juarez: I admire your standing for freedom and right.
Lincoln: Lets shake hands and let's agree we will not stop.
Davis: If we work together, we'll both win this fight.
Max: If we join, then we can come out on top.

Chorus (sung by the spectators):

So take your partner by the hand, [They take their partners by the hand.]
and do the dosey-doe. [They dosey-doe around their partners.]
Sell cotton while you promenade,
make money as you go. [They promenade.]

Then swing your partner round and round,
prepare your guns to roar, [They swing around their partners.]
and slam into the other sets,
and knock them to the floor. [They slam hard into the opposing set.]
[Curtain.]

@@@@@@@@@@@@@

Narrator: Cortina has been leading a number of raids in an attempt to disrupt the flow of Confederate cotton. Also, having declared himself Governor of Tamaulipas, he has taken charge in Brownsville's twin city across the river, Matamoros, in the name of Benito Juárez. Charles Stillman, figuring that Cortina might be interested in raising revenue by collecting tariffs on cotton sent from Brownsville, and recalling that Cortina's mother and other relatives are still living in Brownsville, sends Rip Ford to negotiate with Cortina in an attempt to deal with his more practical side.

@@@@@@@@@@@@@

Act II, Scene 1 – (1863) [Cortina's headquarters in Matamoros. Cortina is sitting at a table across from Rip Ford. Cortina's girlfriend stands behind his chair. Cortina is writing. Then he hands a paper to Rip Ford.]

Cortina: O. K., Colonel Ford. Here's your signed treaty. This allows Stillman and your other Confederate business friends to keep on shipping cotton through Matamoros to the British ships at Puerto Bagdad. Let's drink to it. [The girlfriend serves drinks, and they toast the treaty.]

All: Here's to King Cotton!

Ford: Many thanks. This will give continued prosperity for both Matamoros, and Brownsville. And to show our gratitude, I've been authorized to offer you a commission in the Confederate army with the rank of general.

Cortina: These two intertwined civil wars have brought some surprising developments, I admit. But for me to accept a Confederate commission would be going too far. You Confederates are in cahoots with the French invaders of Mexico. And I am sworn to protect our rightful President, Benito Juarez, and to drive out the French.

Ford: I thought you would say no.

Cortina: The French have already taken over our port of Bagdad. They welcome your trade with the British, and I have just agreed to cooperate with that. But all the same, my main job is to drive them off Mexican soil.

Ford: I can't say I disagree with you on that score.

Cortina: I know about your opposition to monarchy. You cannot be in favor of seeing Mexicans forced to accept Maximiliano as their Emperor.

Ford: No, I don't agree with it.

Cortina: As we Mexicans are saying, "No es un emperador, es un empeorador."

Girlfriend (coarsely): In English that means he's not an emperor, he's just a screw-up.

Ford (snickering): Yeah, I got it.

Cortina: You know, Maximiliano's wife Carlota has said she wants Mexicans to look on her as their mother. So the people are singing: "Adiós, Mamá Carlota, nariz de pelota. La gente se alborota al verte tan gordota."

Girlfriend (giving each word sarcastic emphasis): In English, that means: "Goodby, Mommy of us all, with your nose shaped like a ball. It really drives us up a wall to see you wide as you are tall."

Ford: Yes, I got that, too. Thank you. That's funny. (Heh-heh!)

Cortina: Speaking of walls, I'm really glad that we've torn down the wall between us, Ford, and have been able to co-operate.

Ford: Well, it hasn't been easy, with all the attempts to build walls between the United States and Mexico.

Cortina: The way some people have been talking, you'd think they'd like to build another Great Wall of China along the Mexican-American border!

Ford: That would be pretty silly. Can you imagine it? [They sing…]

Song: The Border Wall

(Sung and danced by Ford, Cortina, and the girlfriend)

Ford: I've got a plan, let's build a border wall. Ha! Ha! Ha!

Cortina: We'll make it high, well over ten feet tall. Ha! Ha! Ha!

Ford: We'll build it through the heart of town.

Cortina (shaking his finger at Ford): Don't you try to tear it down!

Ford: We will hire border guards by millions,
   even though it cost us billions.

Cortina: We'll let it run as far as the eye can see,
   a concrete mess, but that won't bother me.

Ford: No more looking at the river's gliding pace.
   We'll cut off our nose to spite our face.

Ford and Cortina (standing back to back): And we won't see each other
   for all eternity.

Dance: (while Ford and Cortina, standing back to back with their arms out to form a wall, the girlfriend dances on Cortina's side trying to get past the wall, but is blocked by the men's moves right or left every time)

All three sing: We'll let it run as far as the eye can see,
   A concrete mess, but that won't bother me.
   No more looking at the river's gliding pace.
   We'll cut off our nose to spite our face,
   And we won't see each other for all eternity.
   Ha! Ha! Ha! Ha! (They break up laughing) [end of song]

Cortina: Ford, you and I have more in common than I'd like to admit. And I thank you for your protection of my mother through all this chaos, even though she's so mad at me that she's broken off contact.

Ford: Yes, she's pretty angry at your refusal to take back your wife and daughter, as well as at your raiding across the river.

Cortina: Well, try to calm her down.

Ford: I'll do my best.

Cortina: Thanks. [They shake hands.] Here, I'll walk you to the street. [They exit right. The girlfriend looks after them.]

Girlfriend (brazenly, hands on hips): Well, don't get any ideas, Mrs. Goody-goody Mamá Cortina. You are not going to succeed in forcing Cheno back to his wife. He's mine now, and he's going to stay mine. [She sings…]

Song: He'll Always be Mine: Reprise
(Sung by the Girlfriend)

He's had other women. I know what they say.
They all think I'm only his choice for today.
But I've got my eye on him. He won't get away.
He'll always be, always be, always be, always be,
always be, always be mine.
[Spoken during the last two notes] So <u>there</u>!   [Curtain.]

@@@@@@@@@@@@@

Narrator: It is now April of 1864. Union troops have marched from the coast and taken control of Brownsville. They have set fire to Fort Brown and have confiscated all of Charles Stillman's property. Looters and rioters have begun killing people from both sides, and Juan Cortina is right alongside, helping them. Stillman and Glaevecke are forced to flee, but plan to continue transporting cotton into Mexico through Laredo. On the way, they leave Mrs. Glaevecke with Juan Cortina's mother at her ranch.

@@@@@@@@@@@@@

Act II, Scene 2 – (April 1864) [Stillman, Glaevecke, and Mrs. Glaevecke entering left are met by Cortina's mother in front of her Rancho del Carmen ranch house. Mrs. Glaevecke rushes into Mrs. Cortina's arms.]

Mrs. Glaevecke (sobbing): O, Prima! Its all so horrible!

Mrs. Cortina: Come, come, dear!

Stillman: We're all on our way upriver, fleeing for our lives, Mrs. Cortina.

Glaevecke: Ve are stopping here just long enough to leaf my wife vit you. I am sure she vil be safe here.

Mrs. Cortina: The Union troops have chased you out of town?
Glaevecke: *Ja*. Zey marched from ze coast, and took contwol of Bwonsfil.

Stillman: The Confederate soldiers set fire to Fort Brown and to hundreds of valuable bales of cotton waiting to be crossed over to Matamoros.

Mrs. Glaevecke: And that awful fire spread through the whole town. Its such a waste, such a waste!

Mrs. Cortina: (in Spanish) Que horrible!

Stillman: The Yankee forces have confiscated all of our property, and are selling it to the highest bidder. For the time being, we'll use the river crossing at Laredo to get the cotton over to Mexico. That way, our business will go on. The Union army will never force its way that far west.

Mrs. Cortina: Well, Adolphus, you'll find your wife safe here with me when you return.

Stillman: Oh, oh! Listen! [pause] Riders are coming. Come on! Let's get out of here, Glaevecke. [He and Glaevecke rush out.]

Mrs. Cortina: The situation in Brownsville sounds pretty bad.

Mrs. Glaevecke: Nasty men are looting and murdering anyone who gets in their way. They're shouting, "¡Muerte a los gringos!," but they're killing just as many Mexicans as Anglos. And I'm afraid, my dear, that our Cheno is helping them.

Mrs. Cortina: Let me know the worst.

Mrs. Glaevecke: That horrid Union General Herron is even planning a formal banquet to honor Cheno.

Mrs. Cortina: For him and his mistress, I suppose.

Mrs. Glaevecke: Yes, that woman is really showing off, and so is Cheno. He's even renamed Puerto Bagdad as Villa Cortina in his own honor.

Cortina (entering left): I suppose you'd have preferred Villa Glaevecke! My apologies that I didn't consult you first.

Mrs. Cortina: How dare you come on to my property with such arrogant sarcasm, after all of these years of abandoning your family? You've brought us nothing but trouble.

Cortina: I'm sorry, Mamá. I didn't mean to hurt you.

Mrs. Cortina: You're sorry? You expect that lame apology to cover all of these years of heartache? You deserve a good thrashing.

Cortina: Whatever you say. Here. Here is my riding whip. [He hands her the whip, and kneels in front of her.] You can whip me in front of my men, if you see fit. [Mrs Cortina takes the whip and whips him energetically.]

Cortina (surprised by the force of her thrashing): Ow! [softly to himself] That hurt! [Mrs. Cortina throws down the whip with a sob.]

Cortina (standing up and hugging her): O.K. Can you forgive me now?

Mrs. Cortina: No! Things are not all right. You turn your back on your wife and daughter to live with another woman. You shoot people right and left. I hear what's going on. When your fellow General Cobos was issuing orders for prisoners to be executed, why did you tap him on the shoulder, and say, "You first," and have him shot, too?

Cortina: Believe me, it was no great loss.

Mrs. Cortina: A man's life is no great loss? Everyone is a child of God!

Cortina: I knew you were going to get around to religion again! Who are you anyway, Santa Estefana or a society queen?

Mrs. Cortina: I know I'm no saint, and I've been too proud. But I cannot believe your godless life can be making you happy. [She sings…]

Song: That Vacuum in your Heart Wants God

(Sung by Mrs. Cortina)

That vacuum in your heart wants God.
All other fillings are a fraud.
Your moods of desperation
won't find alleviation
until you call upon the Lord.

You think you're just a quirk of fate.
However, it is not too late
to review your situation
and evidence of salvation.
It's worth the effort to debate.

It's easy to deny it.
You do not have to buy it.
You're your own man, your choice is free.
But when you think about it,
You may not want to doubt it.
You're playing with eternity.

Cortina (abrupt): ¡Hasta luego! [He exits. His mother looks after him and sings one last stanza…]

Mrs. Cortina:

You've learned that sinning's not all fun.
It leaves you empty when it's done.
And what about tomorrow?
Don't leave me sunk in sorrow.
I want to see you when our race is run.

Mrs. Cortina [spoken, groaned]: ¡Cheno, mi hijo!

[Curtain.]

@@@@@@@@@@@@

Narrator: The last few months of the two intertwined civil wars in and around Brownsville makes for an intriguing story that is fascinating to all. Listen, now, as our minstrel tells this tale in verse. (One option is to have him tell this to a seated group of children)

@@@@@@@@@@@@

Act II, Scene 3 – The street singer speaks a few lines.

Street singer:

In 1864, in
a sweltering July,
Rip Ford set siege to Brownsville,
for he pledged he would defy
the Yanks who held that city,
to conquer or to die.
The Yanks fled to the Gulf coast,
So they could give another try.

At Rancho del Palmito,
last battle of the Civil War,
not knowing Lee had just surrendered,
the Yanks attacked once more.
Rip Ford held them from Brownsville,
then heard the fight was o'er.
And so he laid his weapons down,
bringing closure to the war.

Stillman wrapped up all his business,
and left from Brownsville while he could.
Cortina lost in Matamoros,
against all likelihood.
He went back to his ranch, where he
resumed his livelihood,
by rustling from the Texans,
who swore to hang him if they could.

[If he is speaking this to children, he might then say, "O.K. kids. Off to bed!]
[Curtain.]

@@@@@@@@@@@@@

Narrator: It is 1877, and Juan Cortina has returned to private life on his ranch outside Matamoros, from where he has continued to carry out cattle raids on the Texas ranches. In April, he is captured and brought before Governor Servando Canales of Tamaulipas, who sentences him to be executed for disrupting border society. When Rip Ford generously intervenes on Cortina's behalf, Canales agrees to send Cortina to Mexico City. There President Porfirio Diaz will commute his sentence to life confinement to Mexico City.

@@@@@@@@@@@@@

Act II, Scene 4: (April 1877) [The office of Governor Servando Canales of Tamaulipas. Cortina stands before Canales with bound hands, while Rip Ford stands watching.]

Canales: Juan Cortina, it was with good reason that you were found guilty of cattle rustling in *Tejas*. Your victims carried their grievances all the way to Mexican President Diaz.

Cortina: I know just what so-called "victims" of mine that would be!

Canales: You have a lot of enemies in Brownsville, but you also have friends there. Colonel John Ford has persuaded me to send you to Mexico City, and let President Diaz decide your fate. I understand he will commute the execution you so richly deserve to life confinement to Mexico City. I don't want to see your face again. [Canales cuts through the ropes around Cortina's hands, throws the rope contemptuously to the floor, and exits]

Cortina: Rip, I've always owed you a lot, but now I owe you my life, too.

Ford: So, you're sentenced to life confinement to Mexico City. It sounds like Br'er Rabbitt thrown into the briar patch to me. [He chuckles.] You'll just have to learn how to live without shooting everything up for a change. I hope you'll forgive my tone of relief when I tell you that Brownsville won't be the same without you.

Cortina: Maybe you'll be able to get a good night's sleep now.

Ford: Well, Brownsville's not the same now anyway. The social scene has lost a lot with the passing away of your charming mother. And Charles Stillman has gone back east, so Brownsville has lost its most visionary patron. And now that you will be away in Mexico City, I'm afraid Brownsville will become a quiet, ordinary town for the first time in its history.

Cortina: Our generation is fading away, all right, both the heroes and the villains.

Ford: Well, maybe we were all of us a mixture of hero and villain. I guess the real culprits were those words "me" and "mine."

Cortina: That's true, but I still have one more little score to settle, with the biggest "me, me, me" of all…Adolphus Glaevecke.

Ford: And how do you plan to settle this score when you're confined to Mexico City? Not with more help from curanderas? [Cortina just laughs.]
[Curtain.]

@@@@@@@@@@@@@@@@@

Narrator: In August of 1879, newspapers as far away as San Antonio are abuzz with the news of how Adolphus Glaevecke's house in Brownsville has been assailed by a poltergeist. Bricks are flying through the air, smashing his house windows, killing his parrot, and driving away the residents, while spectators and Sheriff Brito look on helplessly. No assailant and no source for the bricks can be found, and Juan Cortina is far away in Mexico City.

@@@@@@@@@@@@@@@@@

Act II, Scene 5 – (Monday, 18 August 1879) [Glaevecke's living room in Brownsville. Glaevecke is at the telephone, with Mrs. Glaevecke wringing her hands beside him. The music of "La Curandera Reprise" plays at first.]

Glaevecke (on the phone): Allo! Allo! Perla. Zis is Adolphus Glaevecke again. Sheriff Bwito is still not here. Zis is an emergency. Oh! He is on his vay? Ze bwick twowing is getting worse. I haf been hit, and bwicks are all ofer our floor and yard. Zere's efen a cwowd watching from ze sidewalk.

Mrs. Glaevecke: And tell them that the cook and the other servants have all quit. And one of the bricks hit and killed our poor dear little parrot!

Glaevecke: [Pause.] Tank you. [He hangs up.]

Mrs. Glaevecke: ¡Ay, Dios mío! Who in the world could be throwing these horrid bricks?

Glaevecke: Zey came fwom ze diwection of ze Yznaga's yard, [he gestures to right stage.] but I didn't see anyone zere.

Mrs. Glaevecke: I know it couldn't be one of the Yznagas or their servants. They're always so sweet and nice.

[A barrage of bricks – cardboard bricks can be used – comes through the windows right and hits Glaevecke in the head and shoulder. Mrs. Glaevecke screams. Sheriff Brito knocks at the front door left and is let in by Glaevecke.]

Mrs. Glaevecke: Please, please, do something to stop the bricks, Sheriff.

Brito: We're doing our best. Some people standing on the sidewalk have been hit, too, but nobody can find anybody responsible. [A new barrage of bricks flies through the windows right.] Do you know of any enemy who might be trying to get back at you?

Glaevecke: No. Ze only enemy I hafe who is capable of zis sort of fiolent attack is Juan Cortina. But he has been under city arrest in Mexico City for two years now.

Brito: Well, this is a very curious case. [A new barrage of bricks flies through the windows right. Brito is hit in the body.] Oof! I have all the information I need for now. Good-bye! [Brito rushes out the front door left.]

Mrs. Glaevecke: Adolphus, it must be an evil spirit!

Glaevecke: Vel, I do not belief in poltergeists. [More bricks sail through the windows] *Scheiss Sache!* Let's get out of here.

[Glaevecke runs out, followed by his wife, with bricks flying after them.]
[Curtain.]

@@@@@@@@@@@@

Song: The Waltz of Old Age

(Sung by the Street singer and Chorus in quavering voices while three white-haired old couples painfully and shakily dance a waltz)

With the years passing by came what we might expect,
since the characters didn't die young.
Teeth and hair fell away, as time showed no respect,
and commitments became burdensome.

Our Rio Grande Redbeard became Greybeard instead.
Our Rip Ford the strong became weak.
And Glaevecke's energy, it must be said,
declined quite a bit from its peak.

What's the use of old age, if it only brings loss,
and forgetfulness, worry, and pain?
It should also bring calm so we no longer toss
and turn thinking of setbacks or gain.

If you saw this old set, you'd not reach for your gun.
Nor run to take cover and hide.
But you might be given a lesson hard won,
for kindness had humbled their pride.   [Curtain.]

@@@@@@@@@@@@@

Narrator: In our final scene, the year is 1890. Cortina and his new wife, along with Rip Ford, the Glaeveckes, and others, attend a dinner in honor of Juan Cortina, who has been allowed one brief return visit to Matamoros. Speeches abound, and Cortina fields questions about the 1879 poltergeist, his ideals, and his willingness to forgive his enemies. The men discuss putting aside old animosities and the need for forgiveness between Mexicans and Americans. They envision a day when all of North America will be united in friendship.

@@@@@@@@@@@@@

Act II, Scene 6- (1890) [A restaurant in Matamoros. At a long table, with everybody facing the audience, Cortina sits in the middle, with a new young wife--who is not the previous girlfriend--to his left, Glaevecke to her left, and Mrs. Glaevecke to his left. Rip Ford sits to Cortina's right. Ford rises.]

Ford: Ladies and gentlemen, we have assembled here today to honor a great man, a local legend, and an old friend…Juan Cortina. [Applause, and calls of "Speech! Speech! Ford sits down, and Cortina rises.]

Cortina: Thank you, Rip, for persuading President Díaz to let me come home for this one last visit.

Mrs. Glaevecke: Don't say it's your last visit, primo.

Cortina: I am sixty-six years old, and President Díaz has allowed only this one brief exception to my city arrest in Mexico City. I say, for this last visit. But I want to introduce you to my best discovery in Mexico City – the new Mrs. Cortina. [Cortina sits, and the music plays "He'll Always Be Mine Snippet" as she rises and smiles around the room to applause. Then she sits back down.]

Ford: I would like us to lift our glasses to Juan Cortina the idealist. It is true that for years many of us cursed that day in 1824 when you were born, Juan. We told ourselves that life on the Border would have been so much better without the incessant raids, cattle rustling, battles, and violent deaths. But who else felt so deeply the day-to-day pain of the little man? [Cortina tries to rise, but Ford, behind him, pushes him down.] Who else gave these people a voice? So here's to our local Robin Hood, our Redbeard of the Rio Grande.

[Calls of "To Juan Cortina!" They all lift their glasses and drink. Ford sits down. Glaevecke rises.]

Glaevecke: I know zat you are all surpwised to see me sitting here today side by side with Juan Cortina. Vel, I am ze most surpwised of all. So how did it happen? Only at ze invitation and insistence of Cortina himself. He tells me zat he has forgiven me, and so, den, I forgife him, too. Here is my hand on it, Juan.

[Glaevecke extends his hand to Cortina, who rises and shakes it to applause and cheers.]

Mrs. Glaevecke: Cheno, its so sweet of you to forget and forgive like this. It seems so strange, just like that evil spirit that smashed up our house. If all this were put into a play, the audience would think that it was all made up. [Everyone laughs.]

Glaevecke: Zat reminds me. Cortina, did you arrange zat brick twowing episode zat smashed up my house elefen years ago? Now tell ze twuth!

Mrs. Glaevecke: And if you did, please tell us how you did it. I'm sure that all of Texas would like to know. Even the San Antonio *Daily Express* wrote about it.

Cortina: Oh, let's just let old ghosts fade away.

Ford: Then at least tell us, Juan, what brought you to forgive Glaevecke and your other enemies after all these years?

Cortina: Well, Rip, your saving my life, and your other kindnesses made me rethink what my mother used to say about loving your neighbor as yourself. So here we are. [looking up in the air] I hope she's watching from that Heaven she was so sure of. I hope she's happy with me now.

Ford: May future residents of the Border remember this reconciliation, and take an example from it.

Cortina: Let us drink to brotherhood between our two great peoples!

All (raising their glasses): To brotherhood!

Cortina: We have a powerful and great Hispanic society to the south, and a powerful and great Anglo society to the north. If we don't become brothers, we could pull our continent down into tragedy. But together we could become the happiest continent on earth, and a beacon to the world.

Ford: Yes, but I wonder how this dream of *hermanos unidos* might be realized in practical terms?

Cortina: Maybe one day our Borderland will no longer be the back yards of two countries facing away from each other, but the heart of two nations joined into a true North American community.

Glaevecke: Hey, wait! I'm a proud American, and I don't intend to give that up.

Mrs. Glaevecke: Now, Adolphus, dear! I was a proud Mexican, and I didn't want to give that up.

Cortina: Well, I'm still a proud Mexican, and I will not give that up. But a feeling of pulling together as North Americans does not have to negate our national identities.

Ford: But could our attitudes really change that much?

Cortina: I don't know. I don't know. But if we learn to work together as brothers and sisters in the family of North America, it could be a great blessing to us all.

Song: North America, My Own
(Sung by Cortina, Ford, Glaevecke, Mrs. Glaevecke, and Cortina's wife)

Cortina (stands and sings alone):

North America, my own,
land where global cultures blend
in a link of friend to friend,
I'm proud to claim you for my home.

Ford and Cortina (Ford stands and joins Cortina in a duet):

You're a beauty all the way
from the sea to rolling sea.

Be a homeland for the free
from Panama to Hudson Bay. (Ford waves to Glaevecke to join in singing.)

Verse Three: Glaevecke stands and comes with a cane to join Cortina and Ford in a trio.

Glaevecke, Ford, and Cortina:

Many peoples shaped your rights.
What your early natives started,
Hispanics, French, and Anglos guarded,
whether blacks or tans or whites.

Everybody (standing and singing in a quintet):

God grant our continent new birth
that we hold together sharing,
in a bond of common caring
that will spread through all the earth.

[Curtain.]

@@@@@@@@@@@@@

Song: The Corrido of Juan Cortina: Reprise
(Sung by the Street singer and Chorus)

The Chorus and the street singer (to piano accompaniment):

All you people, come and rally
to the song of Juan Cortina,
from the Rio Grande Valley,
toast of rancho and cantina.

The Street singer (singing alone, playing his guitar):

Where did truth lie in this story?
Who was right, and who was wrong?

But forgiveness brought solution
at the …

Everybody (all instruments joining in the last four words of the song):

… ending of his song.

[End of play.]

THE SCORE FOR PIANO AND VOICE

Overture

Milo Kearney

2003

Corrido of Juan Cortina

Milo Kearney

2003

Cortina Snippet # 1

Milo Kearney

2003

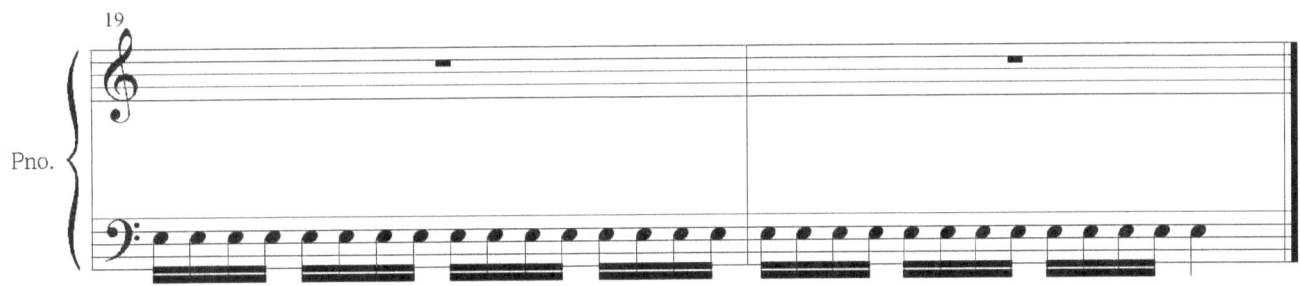

Wedding Processional

Milo Kearney

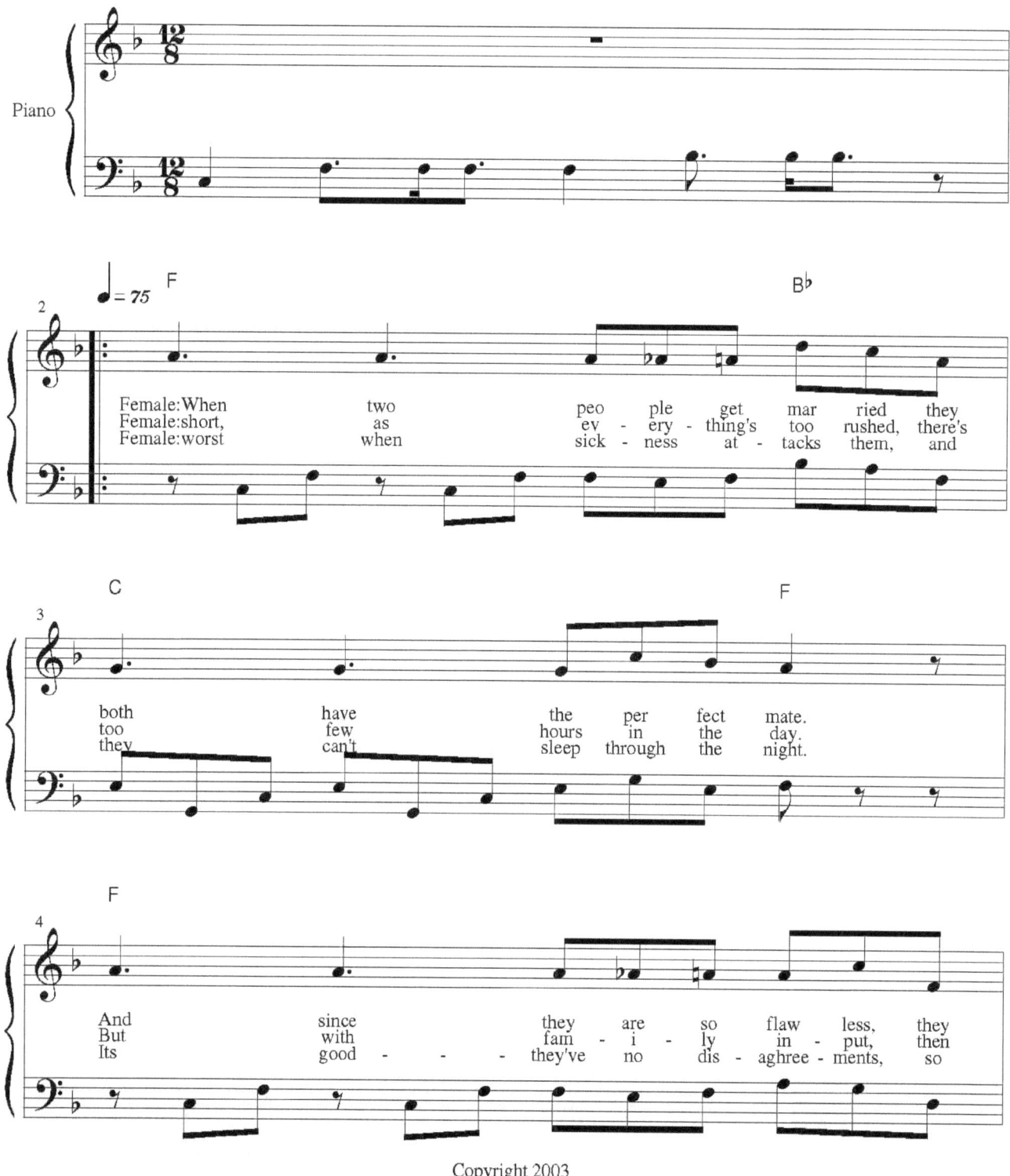

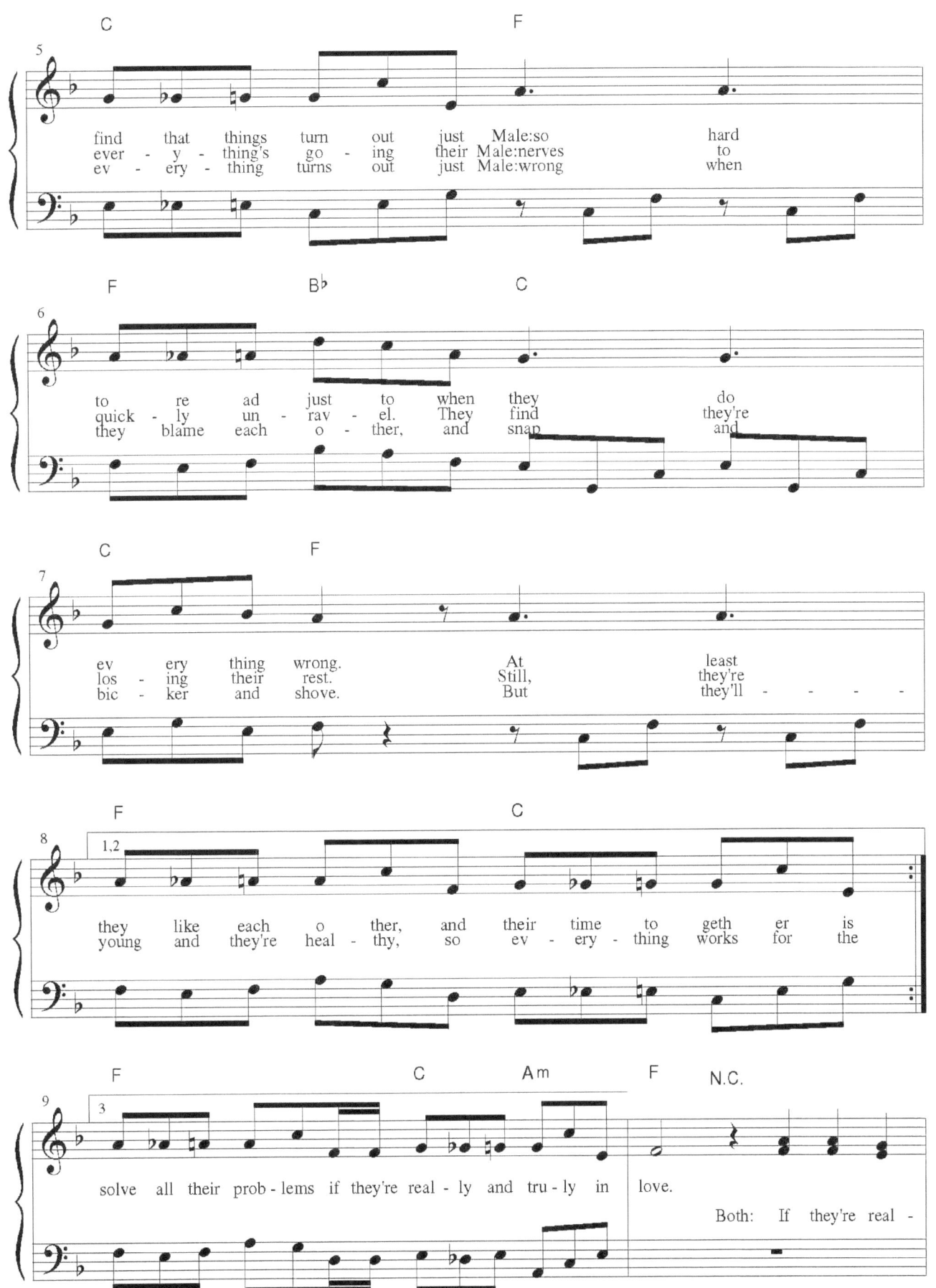

ly   and   tru - - ly   in   love.

He'll Always Be Mine

Milo Kearney

Corrido of Brownsville

Milo Kearney

stand be - side your roads, where
walk - - - - ing in the cold. Win - ter's

Stillman: Palm trees stand   Stillman: side   your roads
Stillman: No more walk - - - -   Stillman: in   the cold

flocks   of   birds have their a - bodes.
no   wonder - land   when you   grow old.

Stillman: birds have their a - bodes.
Stillman: land   when you   grow old.

My   dear
My   dear

Society Queen of Brownsville

Milo Kearney

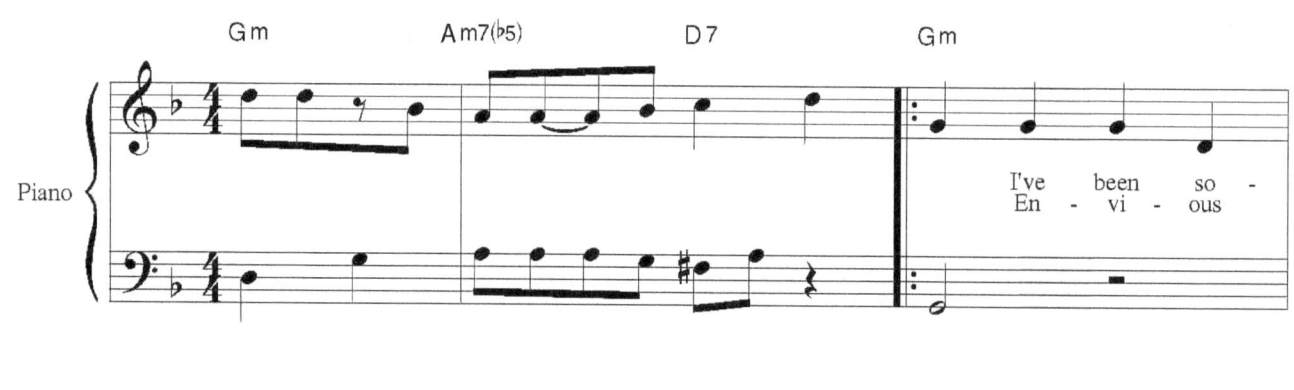

I've been so -
En - vi - ous

ci - e - ty Queen for years now. I set the tone as you will al -
peop - le are left to stew, one step be - hind me or ev - en

low. I've held on - to my po - si - tion some - how. I'm still the
two. They would re - place me that much - is true. But they just

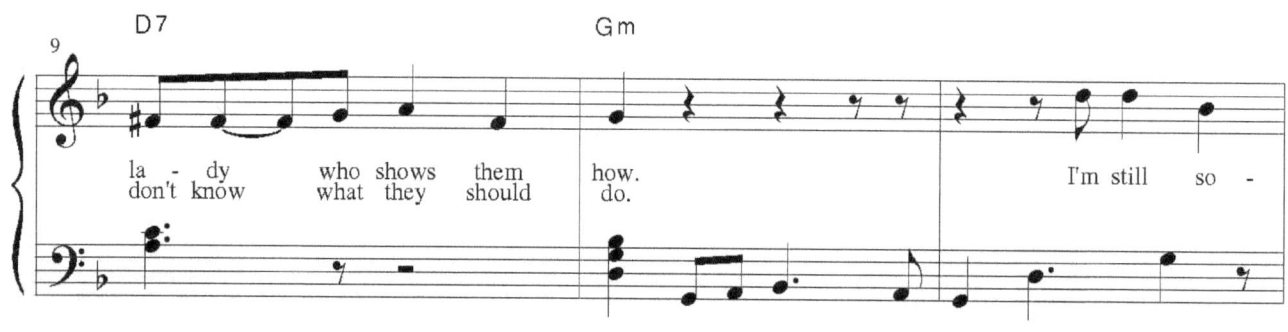

la - dy who shows them how. I'm still so -
don't know what they should do.

Slippery Slope

Milo Kearney

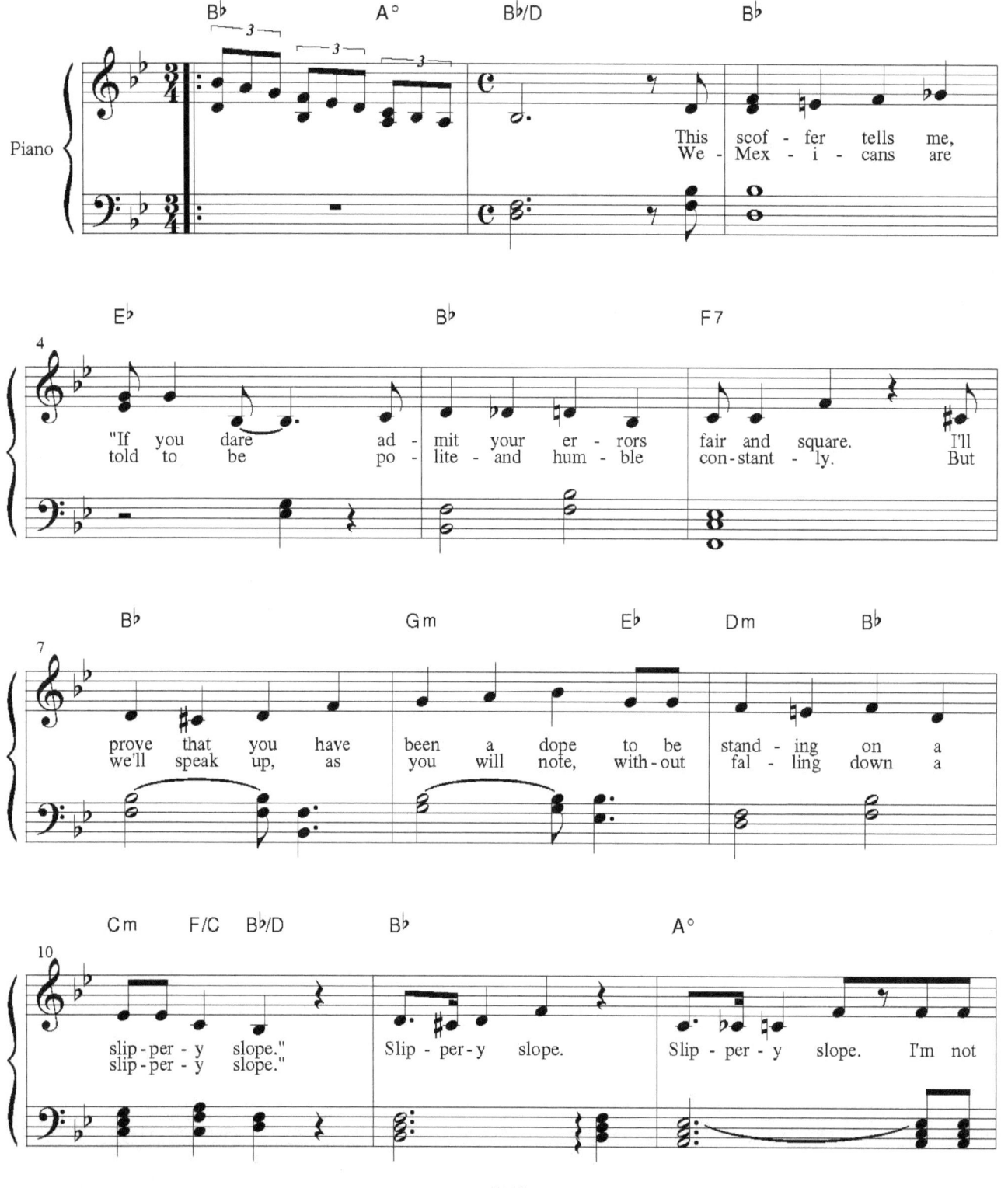

2005

think it through, the light will come to you. You'll see I'm stand-ing-on the rock of

fair - - - - - - - ness.

Am I a Mexican or an American?

Milo Kearney

can.   On the oth - er hand. Am I a   Me   -   xi -

can,   or A - mer   -   i - can,   when   all   is   said - and

done?   Am I a   Me - xi - can?   or an Am - er - i -

can?   I'd   like   to   know   which   one.   I   buy U. S.

can, right? Then I must be an A-mer-i - can. I'm fri-

jo - les and ham-bur-ger, som - bre - ro and jeans, nor - te - no and

South-er - ner, such a mix - ture of things! So, if I walk like a

Mex - i-can, and talk like an A-mer - can, and walk like an A-mer - i -

can,   and talk   like - a   Mex - i - can,   am I a

Mex - i-can?   Or am I A - mer - i-can?   Cabrerra: I   guess you're both, Jefe. Cortina:

No!   Carramba!   I'm   still a Mex   -   i - can!

La Curandera

Milo Kearney

We'll lis - ten to the fates you tell.
Are you the hea - ler or the plague?
For he is wait - ing to be told.

Ooo - ooo - ooo -
Ooo - ooo - ooo -
Ooo - ooo - ooo -

ooo - ooo - ooo - ooo - ooo - ooo.
ooo - oo - oo - oo - oo - ooo.
ooo - ooo - ooo - ooo - ooo - ooo.

Dm   Cm   A°   Gm   N.C.

Ballad of Cortina the Hero

Milo Kearney

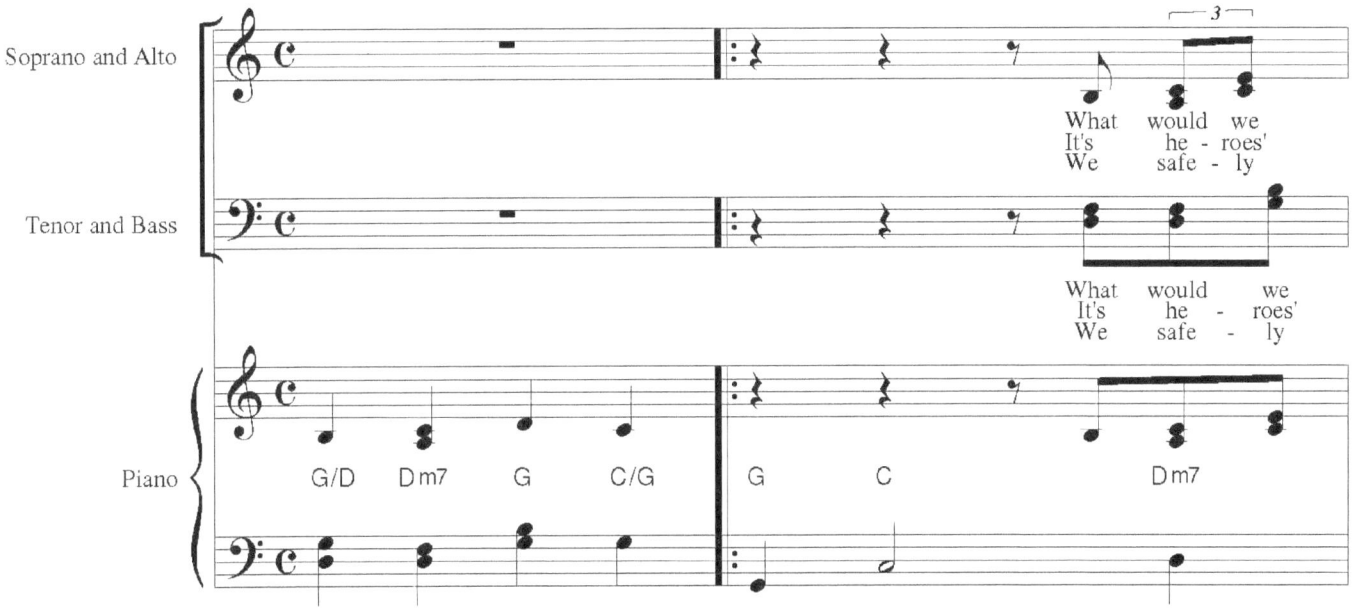

2003

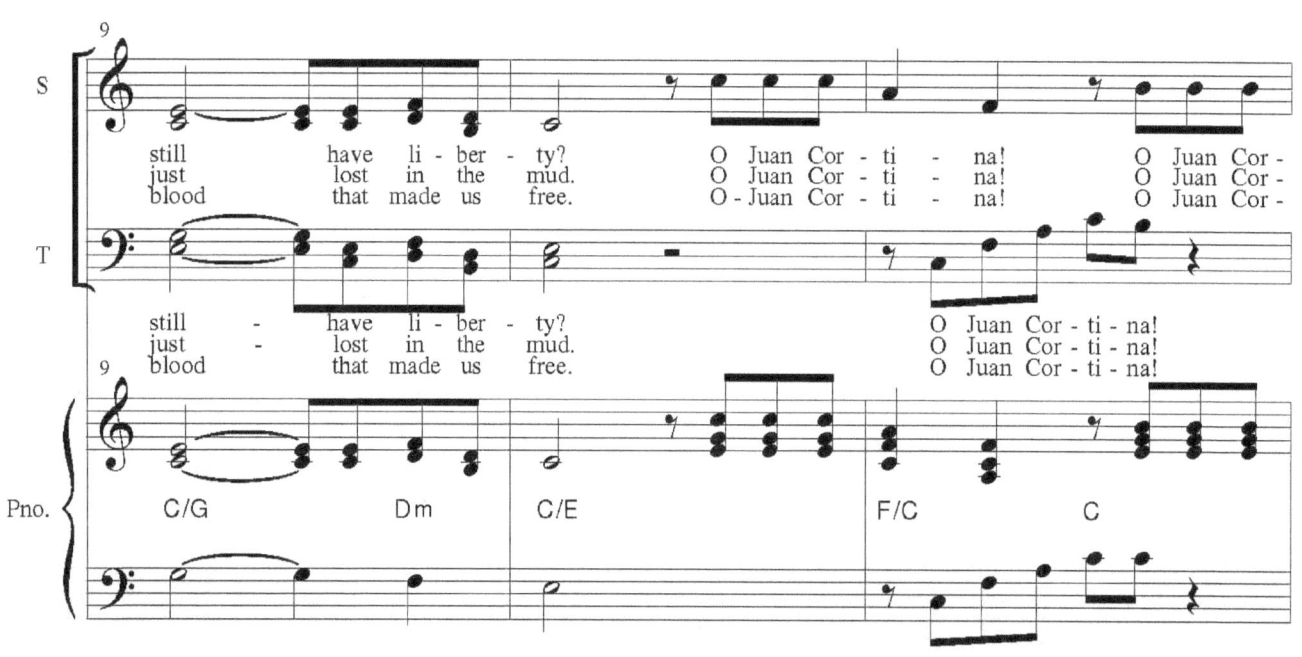

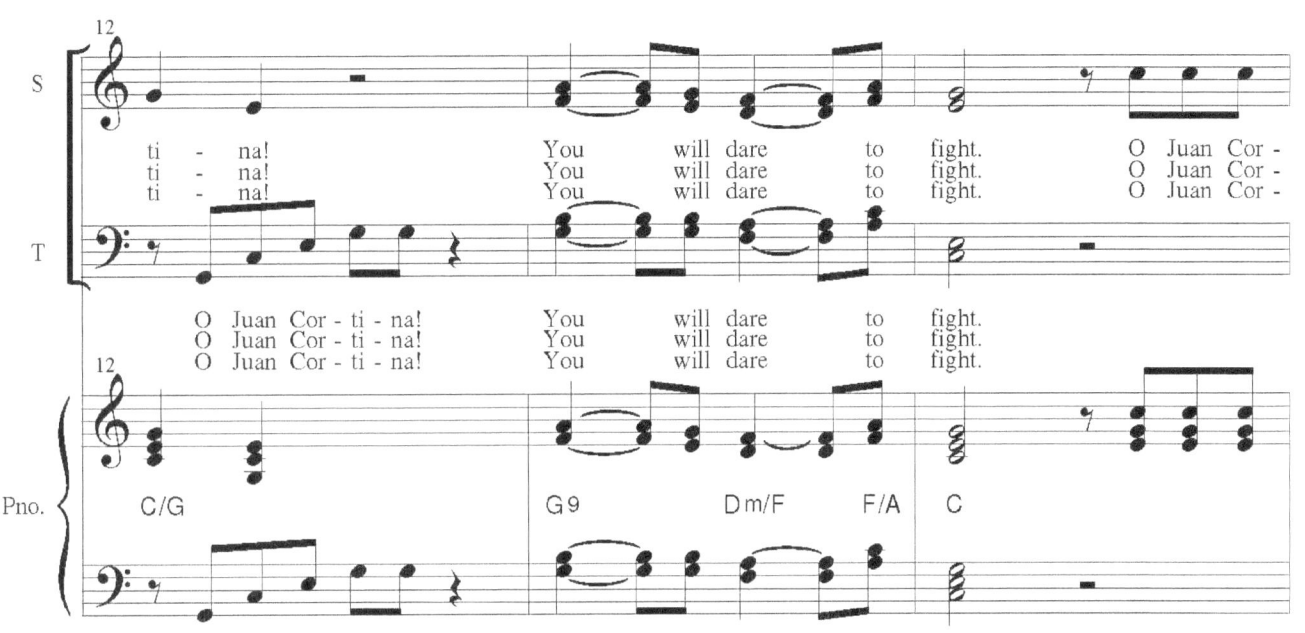

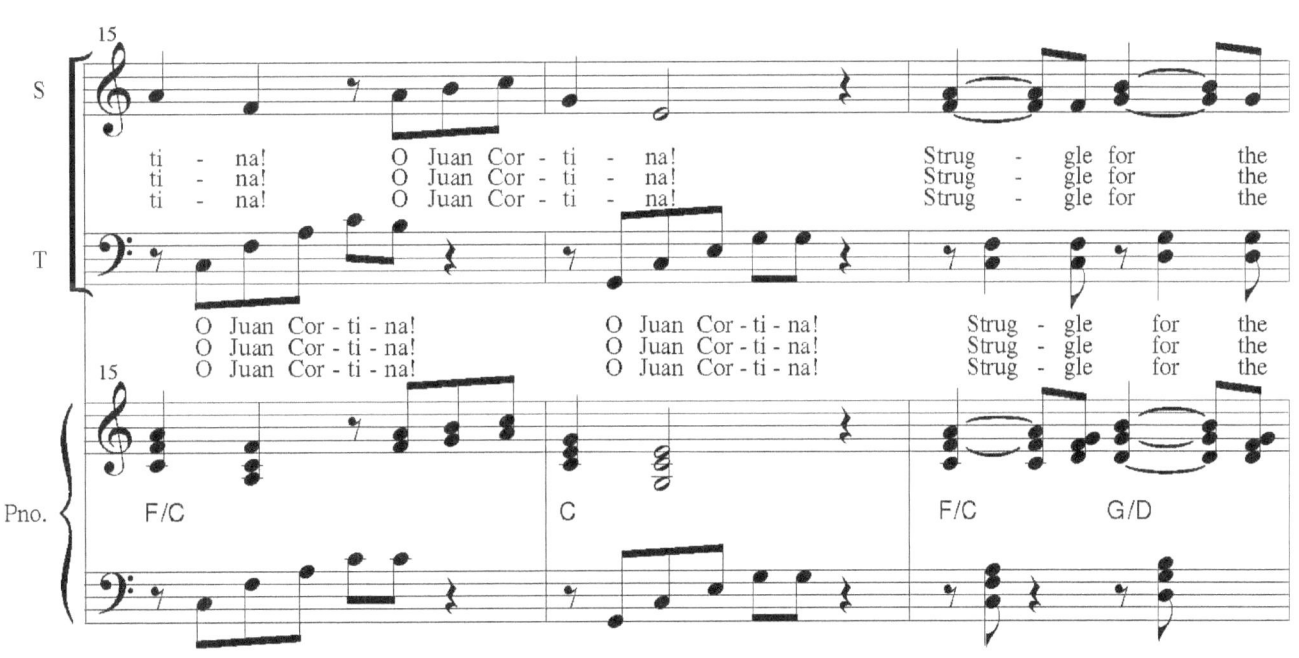

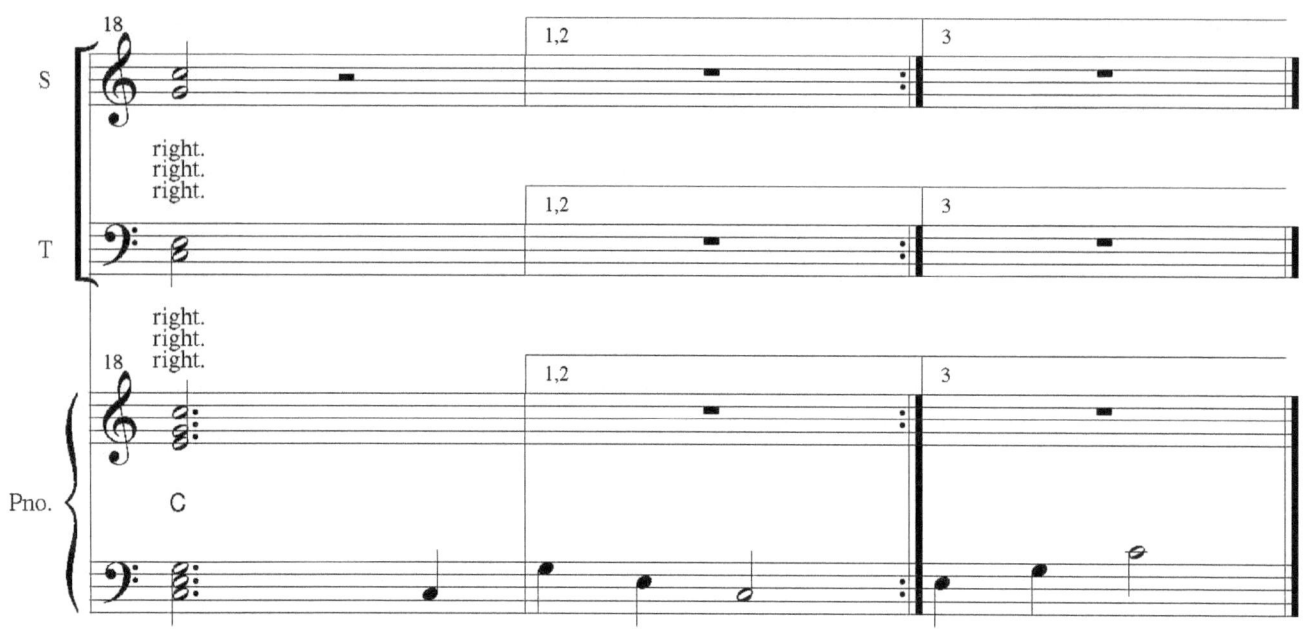

Cortina Snippet # 2

Milo Kearney

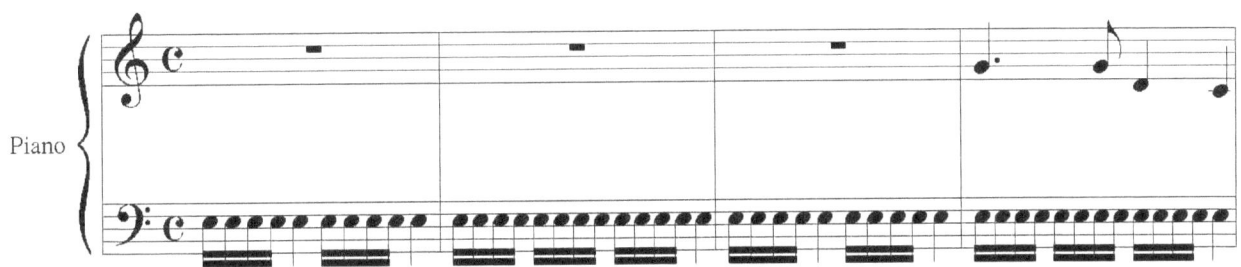

2003

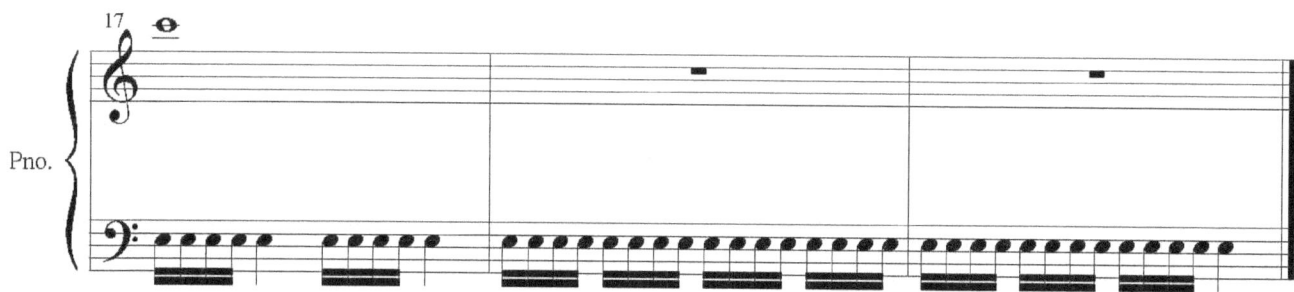

Did It Have To End Like This?

Milo Kearney

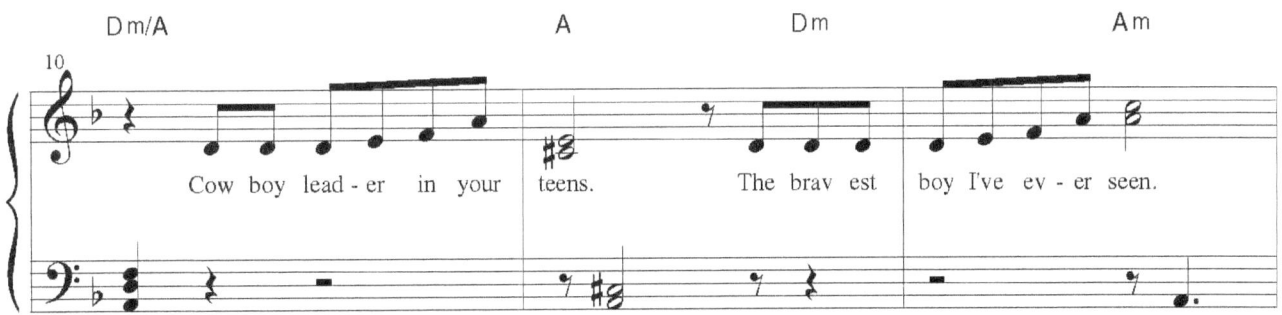

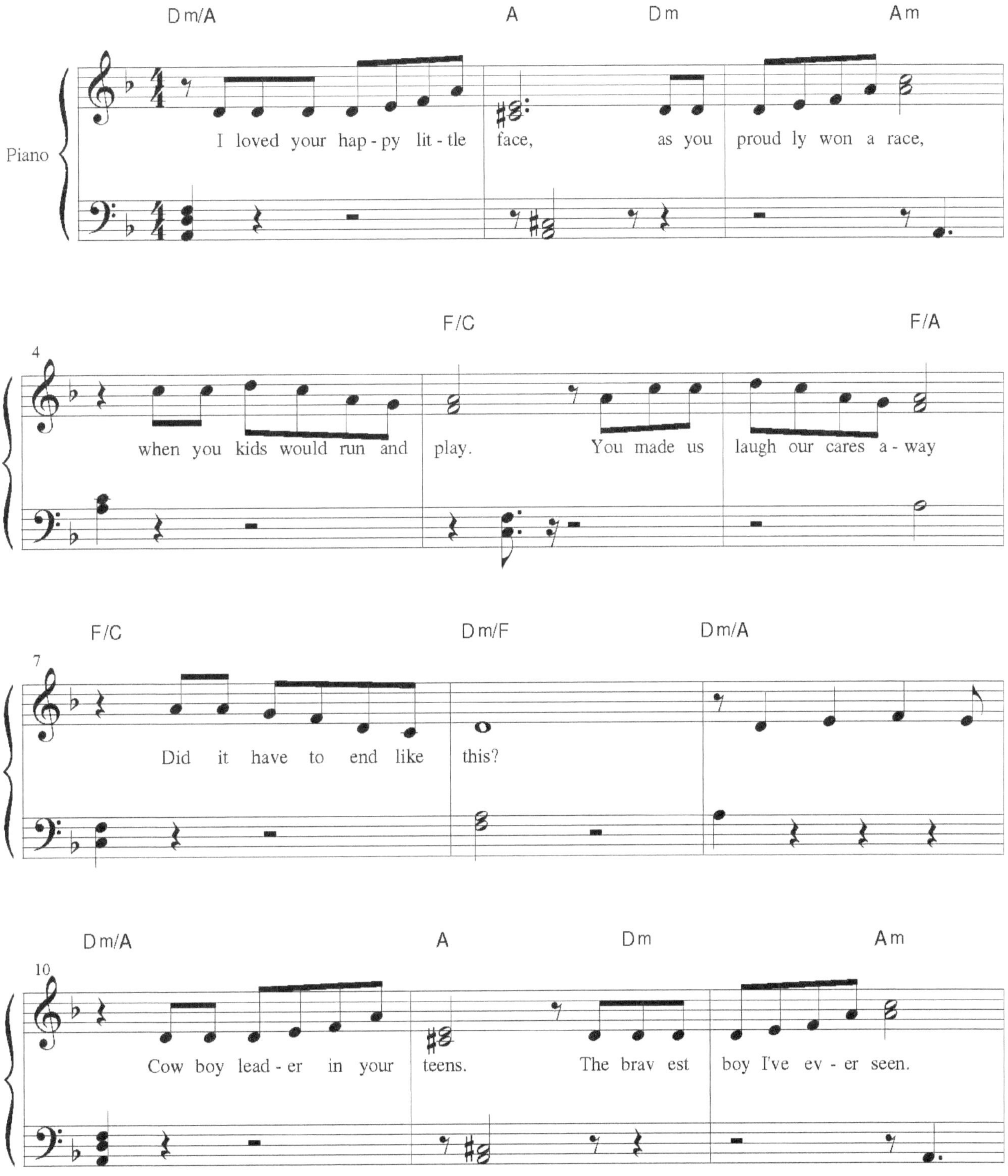

Dm/A
A
Dm
Am
Piano
I loved your hap - py lit - tle face, as you proud ly won a race,
4
F/C
F/A
when you kids would run and play. You made us laugh our cares a - way
7
F/C
Dm/F
Dm/A
Did it have to end like this?
10
Dm/A
A
Dm
Am
Cow boy lead - er in your teens. The brav est boy I've ev - er seen.

We'll Be Back

Milo Kearney

2006

Square Dance of the Civil Wars

Milo Kearney

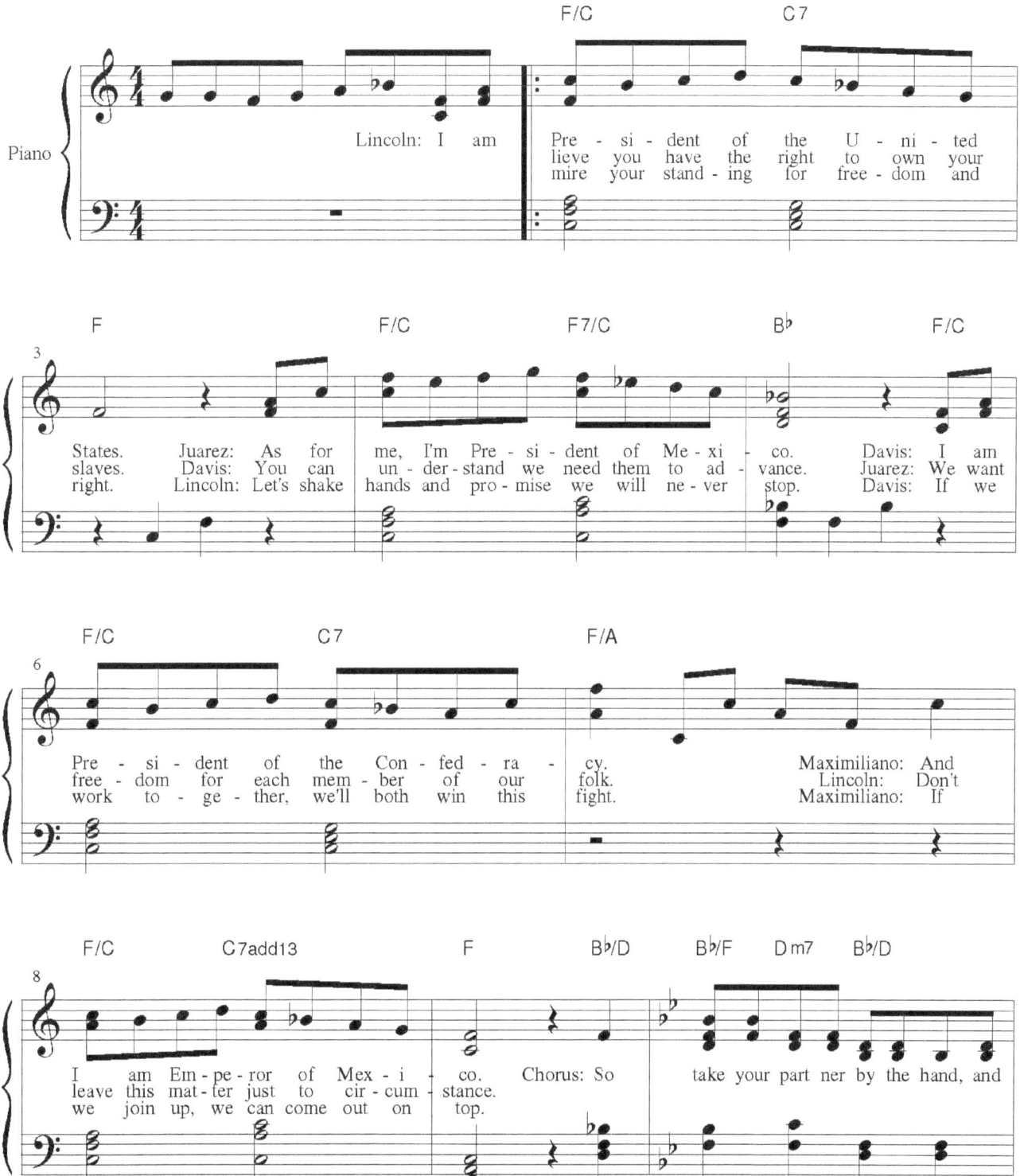

The Border Wall

Milo Kearney

2008

way that it will be. (Dance of trying to get past the wall)

Ford, Cortina, and girlfriend: We'll let it run as far as the

eye can see, an ug-ly mess, but that won't bo - ther me. No more

He'll Always Be Mine Reprise

Milo Kearney

He's had o-ther wo-men, I know what they say. They all think I'm on-ly his choice for to-day. - But I've got my eye on him, he won't get a-way. He'll al-ways be, al-ways be, al-ways be, al-ways be, al-ways be, al-ways be mine.

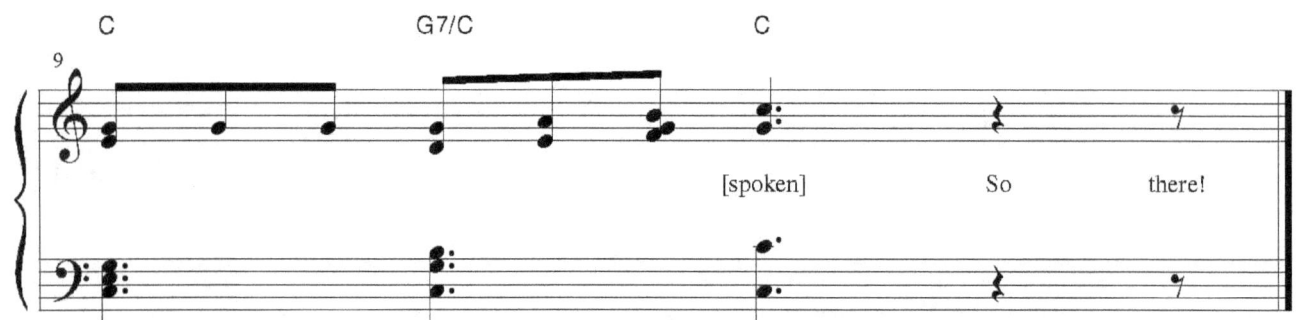

[spoken]   So   there!

That Vacuum in Your Heart

Milo Kearney

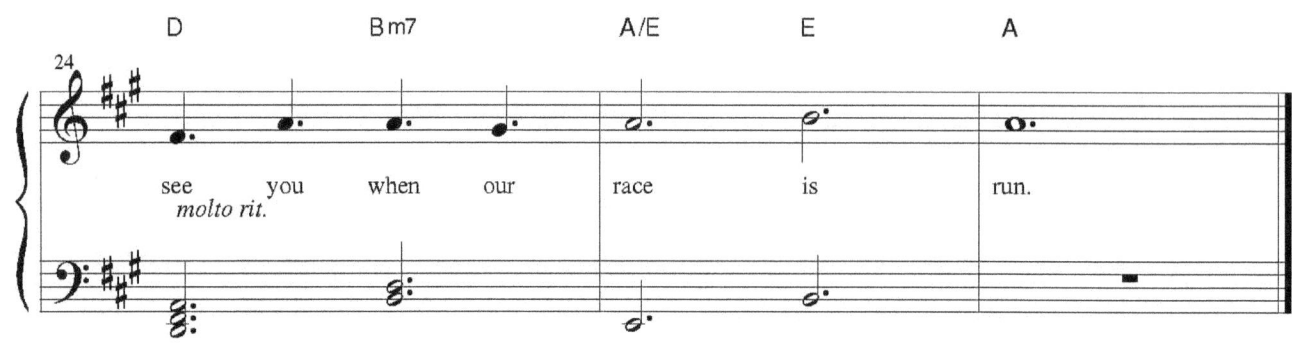

see you when our race is run.

La Curandera Reprise

Milo Kearney

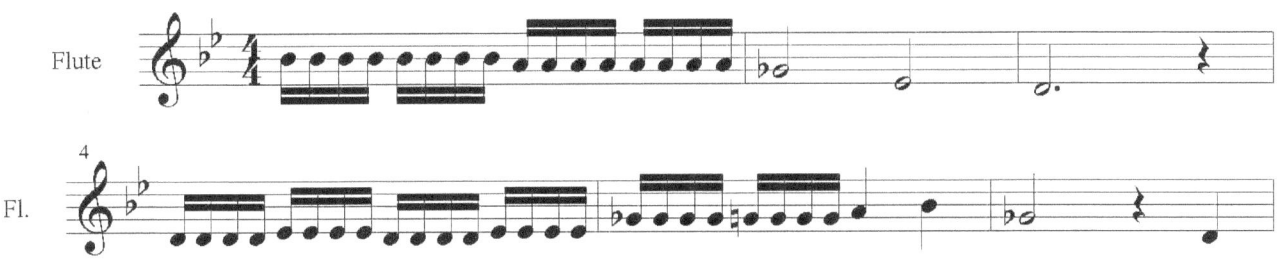

2003

The Waltz of Old Age

Milo and Vivian Kearney

beard be-came grey beard in - stead. Our Rip Ford the Strong be came weak.
set, you'd not reach for your gun, nor run to take co - ver and hide.

And Glae - vec - ke's en - er gy, it must be said, de - clined quite a
But you might have been gi - ven a les - son hard won, for kind - ness had

bit from its peak. - rit. -
hum - bled their pride. - rit. -

He'll Always Be Mine Snippet

Milo Kearney

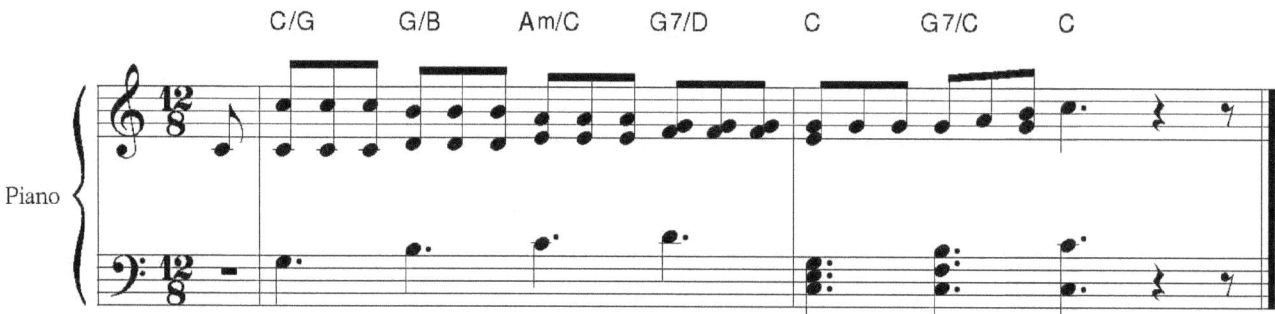

North America, My Own

Milo Kearney

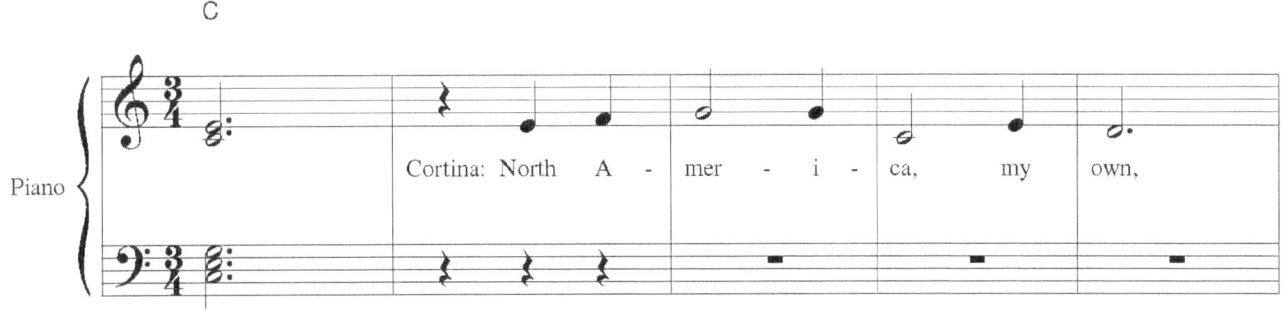

Cortina: North A - mer - i - ca, my own,

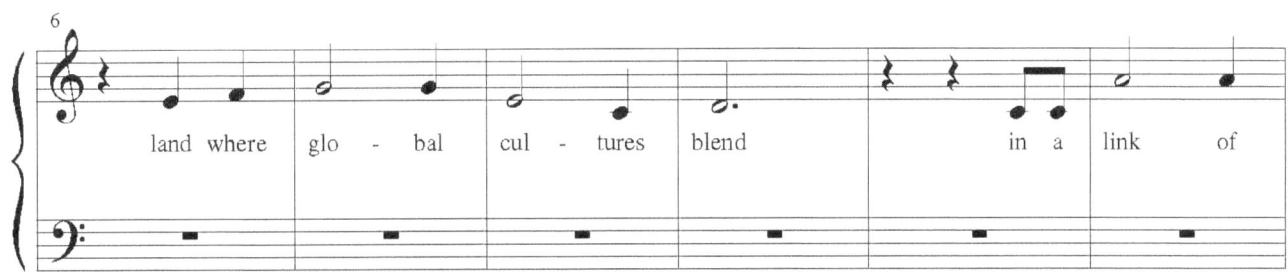

land where glo - bal cul - tures blend in a link of

friend to friend, I'm proud to claim you for my

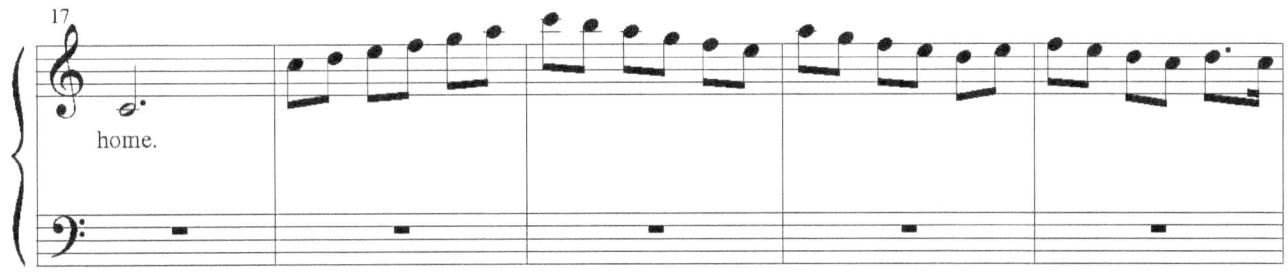

home.

Cortina/Ford/duet: You're a beau - ty all the way

from the sea to rol - ling sea. Be a - home - land

for the free From Pa-na-ma to Hud - son Bay.

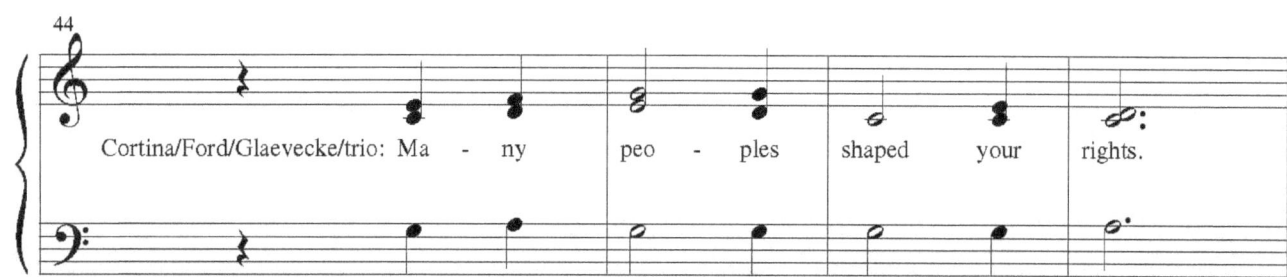

Cortina/Ford/Glaevecke/trio: Ma - ny peo - ples shaped your rights.

What your ear - ly na - tives star - ted His - pan - ics,

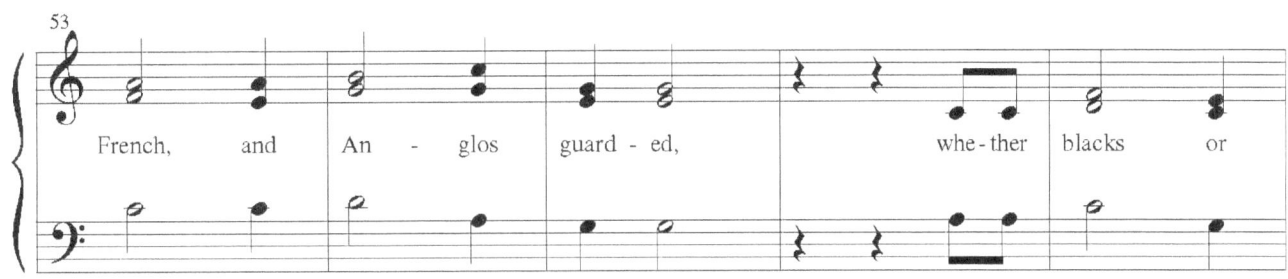

French, and An - glos guard - ed, whe - ther blacks or

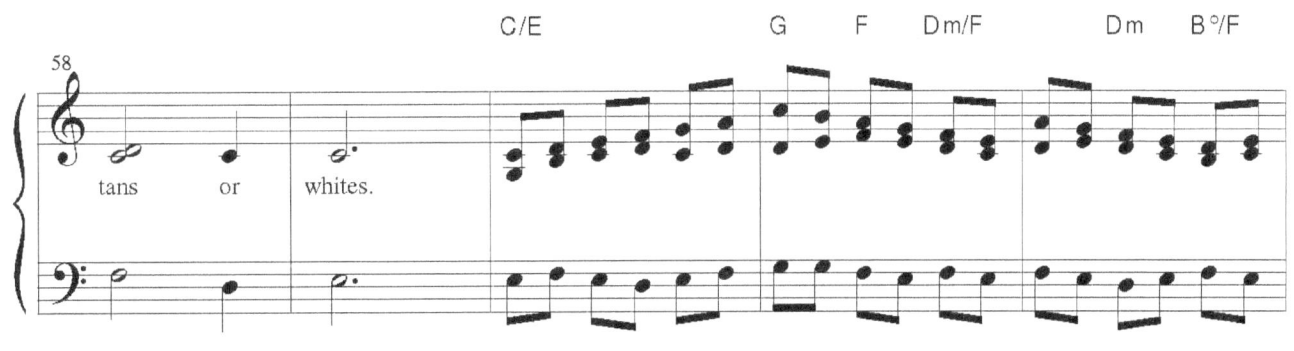

C/E   G   F   Dm/F   Dm   B°/F

tans or whites.

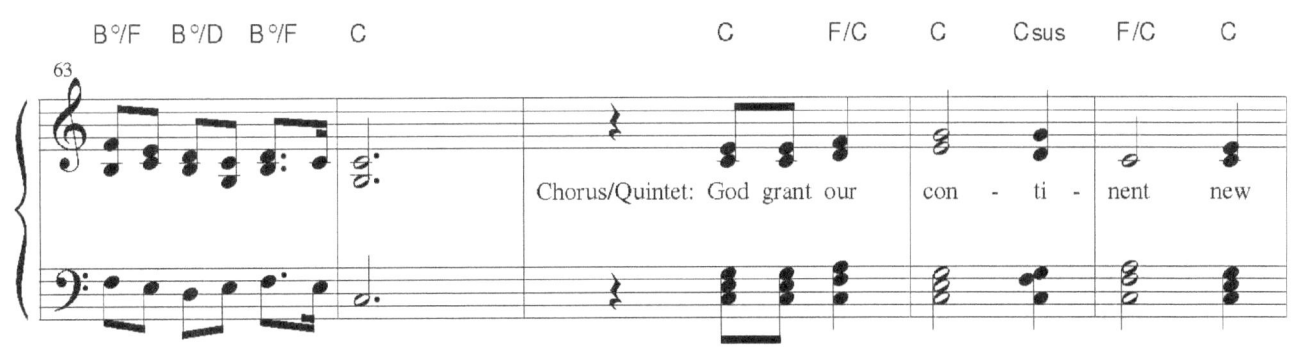

B°/F   B°/D   B°/F   C   C   F/C   C   Csus   F/C   C

Chorus/Quintet: God grant our con - ti - nent new

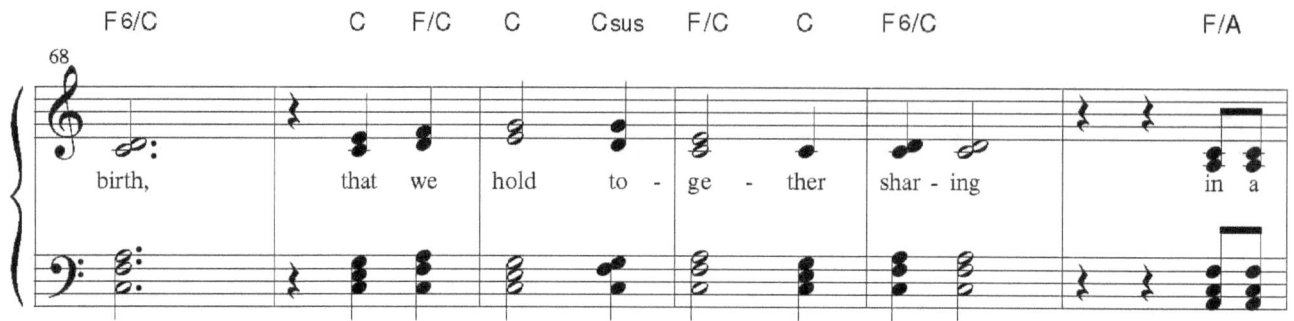

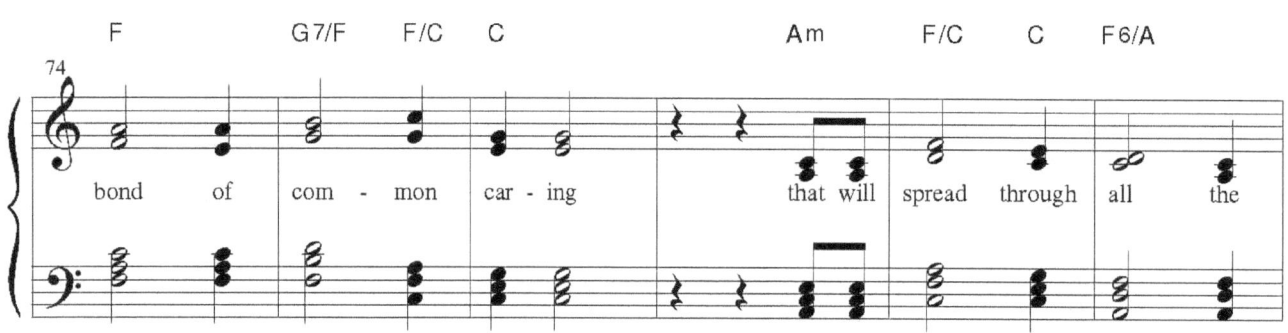

The Corrido of Juan Cortina Reprise

Milo Kearney

Chorus: All you peo-ple, come an ral-ly to the song of Juan Cor-ti-na, from the

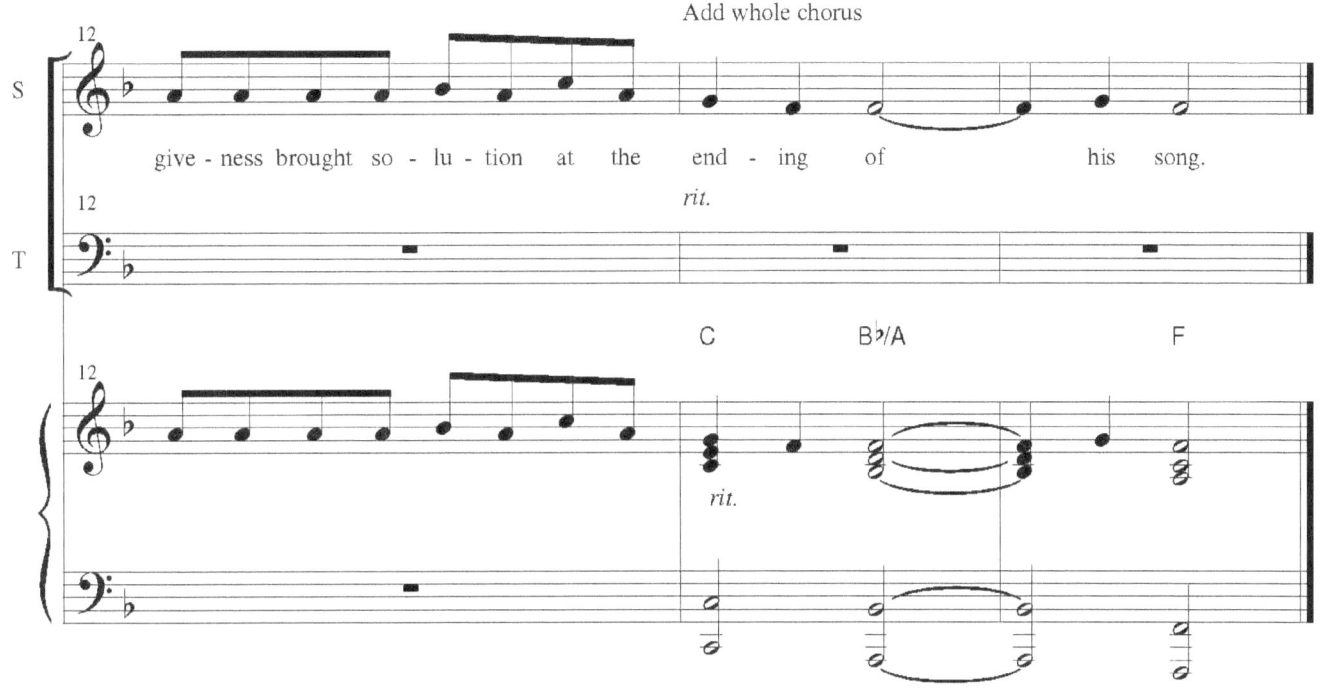

give - ness brought so - lu - tion at the end - ing of his song.

www.ingramcontent.com/pod-product-compliance
Lightning Source LLC
Chambersburg PA
CBHW081154170626

46813CB00009B/3188